The Following Sea

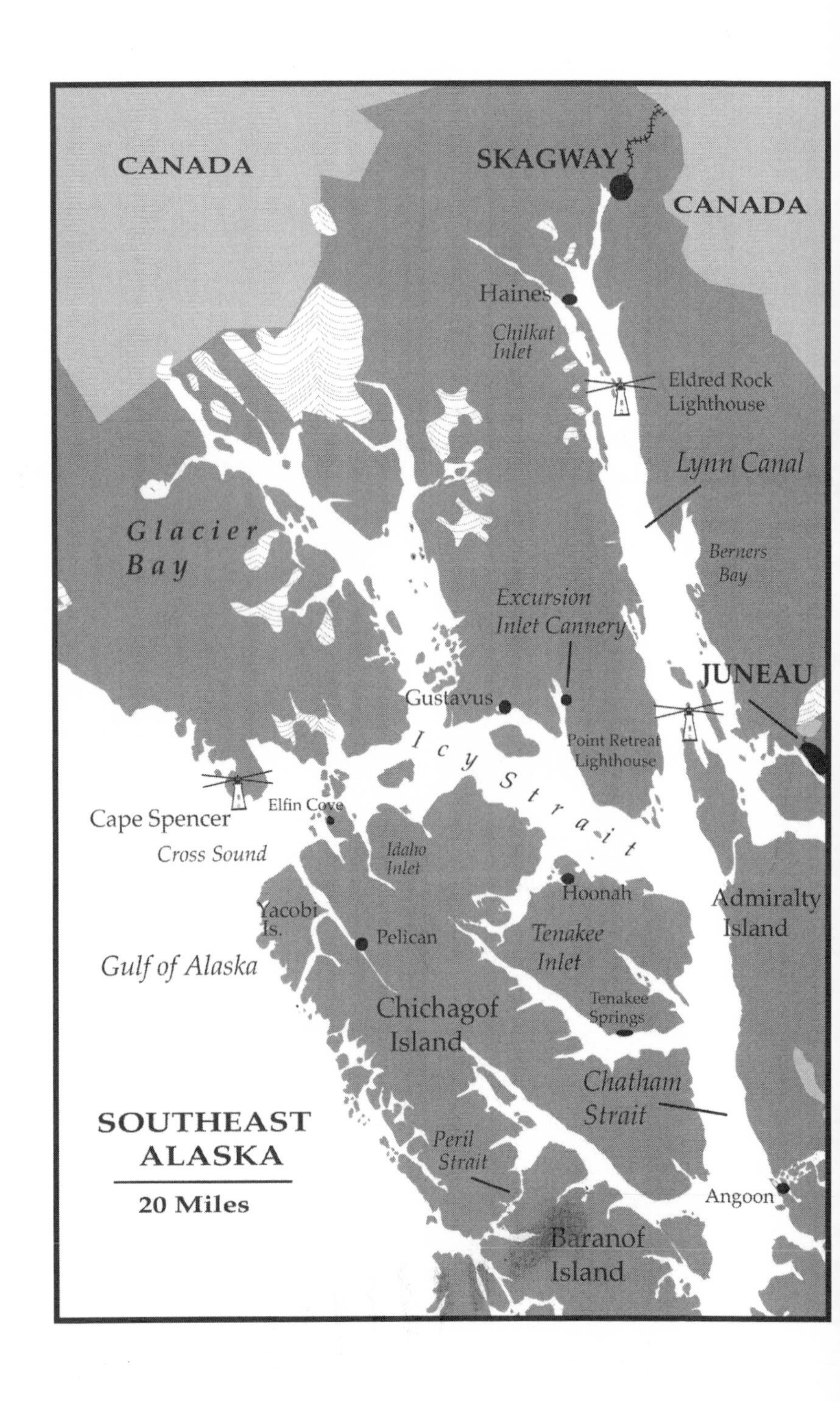
CANADA
SKAGWAY
CANADA
Haines
Chilkat Inlet
Eldred Rock Lighthouse
Lynn Canal
Glacier Bay
Berners Bay
Excursion Inlet Cannery
JUNEAU
Gustavus
Point Retreat Lighthouse
Icy Strait
Cape Spencer
Elfin Cove
Cross Sound
Idaho Inlet
Hoonah
Admiralty Island
Yacobi Is.
Pelican
Tenakee Inlet
Gulf of Alaska
Chichagof Island
Tenakee Springs
Chatham Strait
SOUTHEAST ALASKA
20 Miles
Peril Strait
Angoon
Baranof Island

The Following Sea

Marcel Jolley

Black Lawrence Press

Black Lawrence Press
www.blacklawrence.com

Executive Editor: Diane Goettel
Cover design: Pam Golafshar
Book design: Amy Freels

Map by Joe Upton

ISBN: 978-1-937854-30-0

Published 2013 by Black Lawrence Books, an imprint of Dzanc Books
Printed in the United States

For my mother and father

The previous spring Joseph Merickel tracked a dead moose for almost two days. Seven months later people still debated how the animal met her end. Some said a state ferry hit her when she was swimming, while others speculated she was poached on shore from a passing fishing boat but fell in somewhere unrecoverable. Whatever her origin, the waterlogged cow rode the tides to Skagway's harbor where she surprised an underwater welder down for his first dive of the day working on the new railroad dock. After the shock wore off, the welder and his partner dragged the moose out with a come-along and deposited her in a friend's driveway before breakfast. In the flat grey of that March morning this appeared a great practical joke, and the friend no sooner discovered the moose than perpetuated the prank on a neighbor.

Word eventually reached Chief of Police Merickel, who recognized the caper to be if not illegal at least in bad taste. The citizenry's thawing sense of humor kept the moose agile, but Merickel cornered her the next afternoon on the school superintendent's lawn, where deceased animals and juvenile antics alike ground to a halt. No charges were filed and several participants volunteered to haul the carcass to the dump. Everyone shared a good chuckle and the *Anchorage Daily News* awarded the tale top billing in their *Life* section.

Now Linda Walker lay dead in her rented cabin off the Dyea Road with bruises suggesting struggle and blunt force trauma. Her boyfriend Scott Sounder was nowhere around. Officer Lambar could be heard retching out back. This first Thursday of October 1994 was barely seven hours old, but promised to be the town's fourth day of heavy rain. There was no good day for this, but it being a Thursday somehow made Merickel feel worse.

He stood on the porch while drops rang the surrounding canopy of trees like the old ball diamond's flattop dugouts. Merickel had seen people lose much more blood and still live, but checking for a pulse and dialing the fire department had taken everything in him. Already he heard the ambulance's wail down in town. Were he to walk back past Lambar, the cabin's hillside perch would allow an unhampered view of Skagway's small grid of streets and the rig northbound for the bridge. But the siren meant movement, which in turn meant no more than ten minutes.

"Yeah, I just peered in and…shit, you see."

Karl Deem's voice made Merickel start as the man emerged onto the porch. As much of a slumlord as a population of seven hundred allowed, Deem had come by earlier that morning for the overdue rent, likely hoping to catch Linda in the shower. Between Linda and his vomiting junior officer, Merickel had lost track of the old man.

"Probably best not to poke around in there, Karl. Being a crime scene and all."

"It's my damn place." Deem snorted but knew his error. "You should string up your yellow tape if that's the case."

Merickel recalled last seeing his own roll in the bottom desk drawer with a day planner still wrapped in cellophane.

"Just stick by me for now, okay?"

The EMTs left their siren on until the ambulance stopped, the hood steaming as the engine ticked down. The full-time guy was accompanied by a volunteer of about twenty-two who wore his work coveralls under one of the heavy orange jackets bought with profits from the department's 4th of July barbeque. Deem followed them in but Merickel waited on the porch until he heard the young part-timer radioing the clinic. The kid stood over Linda, struggling with syntax as if any error would worsen her fate.

"...got a female with signs of strangulation and hits," he said. "Or contusions, I mean. Looks to be in her late thirties..."

"Thirty-six," Merickel said.

Both EMTs looked up.

"Linda was thirty-six. Would have been thirty-seven next January," he said. "I only know because her name falls on the same month as mine on the community calendar."

One such calendar, put out by the Emblem Club and bearing the birthday of anyone willing to pay the five-dollar fee, hung on the fridge. Merickel pointed but the EMTs only stared. A crackling female voice over the radio asked if they were still there.

"So, yeah, she was thirty-six."

* * *

During the five minutes needed to confirm Linda was dead Merickel busied himself with the department Polaroid normally used to catalog dogs at large, closing his eyes before each shot. Lambar had recovered but stayed outside. He kept his own police tape in the glove box but was unfamiliar with the process, and Merickel emerged to a yellow web screaming against the dirt driveway.

"I guess that about does it for now." Merickel pocketed the Polaroids without waiting for them to develop. The EMTs retrieved a black bag and stretcher while he stepped up beside Lambar. The kid lost two of his twenty-three years to the snug uniform and one more to a soft farm-boy face.

"I'm sorry, Joe. That wasn't professional at all."

Merickel started to put a hand on his shoulder but stopped just short of contact. "Don't worry. She was my friend, too."

Lambar had been sweet on Linda in a futile way that five years earlier could have legally been termed a schoolboy crush. He had come north last December from Colorado, where a decade before Linda had attended flight school. The two often spoke of life down south and played volleyball Thursday nights at the gym, though Merickel knew Lambar was a bigger fan of Linda than of volleyball.

A clanking on the step got their attention. The EMTs had misjudged the doorway's drop, and after a sheepish look focused all energies on getting Linda to the ambulance with no more trouble. Merickel offered a solemn wave when they drove off with no siren but bulbs popping.

"Why don't you run me to city hall for my cruiser," Merickel said. "Then I'll come back for another look around. You can start tracking down kin and making calls." He could see only a few hundred feet up the mountain, where low clouds waited to settle into the trees. No planes again today. "See who Canadian customs has had come up the highway lately. I'll check the ferry."

Merickel retrieved Deem, who looked to be in search of a rent check thoughtfully filled out beforehand. After locking the door, the landlord surrendered his key with a smirk.

"I bet you're going to say I'm not allowed back in my own cabin, eh?"

Merickel said he was afraid so and watched Deem disappear down the snaking road without a blink of taillights or passing nod at the posted limit. Moments later the lawmen followed in Lambar's Isuzu Trooper cruiser. Rain overflowed the ditches and pulsed across the pavement in thick veins.

"That bastard." Lambar accompanied his outburst with an open palm against the steering wheel. Merickel just studied the water.

"So you think it was Scott."

Lambar winced at having thrown himself into a test.

"I don't *know* that, but if I had to guess..."

"I'm pretty sure you're right," Merickel said, mostly to relax the young officer. "Still, we need to move carefully. News will run through town like a good flu. I don't recall seeing one of Westwind's planes at the airport but let's swing by anyway. And I need you to call Johnny Lester in Juneau. Tell him I'll be in touch later today, tonight at the latest."

Linda and Sounder were—or had been—pilots for Johnny's Westwind Airways. Although based in Juneau eighty miles to the south, Linda maintained her cabin here and Johnny often let her make the last Skagway run of the day and keep a plane overnight. Merickel had known Johnny for eighteen years and though news of a deceased employee should probably come from a friend, he hoped this might go down easier via an official stranger. He had watched the Army do things that way for twelve years and they had far more experience with dead people.

Crossing the bridge Lambar turned onto the lone remaining gravel street that hugged the river down to the airstrip. Sure enough, no Westwind aircraft, just a stable of Skagway Air Service Cherokees and a few private airplanes slick with rain. Merickel returned a few morning waves as Lambar rolled them toward city hall, offering each a tight smile. They would know soon enough. This was the town's first killing in a long haul, and when things didn't hit often they hit hard. Lambar stared forward out of what his chief assumed some misguided sense of respect. His eyes were red from more than a good puke and Merickel couldn't begrudge him. Crushes made guys cry even when the girl was alive.

Even through a water-streaked windshield Merickel noticed his own Isuzu Trooper listing to port as they approached city hall. Both left tires slouched flat, a quick inspection revealing them deflated via the valve stem.

"Calhoun?" Lambar said.

"Most likely."

The review committee for the chief of police position did not meet for another six weeks, but campaigning appeared to be underway. Merickel would not be surprised to find honest slashes by Halloween.

* * *

Ever prepared, Lambar kept two cans of Fix-A-Flat in his Isuzu, supplying Merickel enough pressure for a wobbly trip to PetroMarine's air pump. He drove next down to the ferry terminal, an indignant middle finger in the hand of piers reaching south after cruise ships now a month gone. A handwritten sign in the window confirmed the terminal was closed and would remain so until the Friday afternoon boat. The lot was empty and Merickel could not imagine a criminal stupid enough to rely on the state ferry for escape, but he made a note to call the terminal manager and see if Scott Sounder had been on any recent sailings. The Burro Creek fish hatchery lay visible across the bay but beyond that the clouds and inlet melted into bruised greys and blues. A nearby viaduct pumped a thick vein of brown runoff, and the river and streams ran bloated to a point that demanded notice. All of this was standard for fall, but even a boxer fully aware of having been beaten up the night before still startled at the first reflection of his swollen face.

The dash clock read just after eight a.m. Jan would still be readying the kids for school. She had to have realized something was not right when Lambar came by early to pick him up this morning, but she would want to know more than he knew right now. So Merickel drove back to the cabin.

The lot was prime real estate, especially with all of the valley's usable land below bought up by longtime locals or summer tour outfits. The cabin's heavy log walls and low ceiling wrapped around anyone who entered like a homemade quilt. The living room, kitchen and bedroom blended together, delineated only by strategic plants and a bookcase. A lone additional door led to the cramped afterthought bathroom. The bed's overflowing comforter, save for a few browning stains, invited a soul to dive in.

Many of the books might have belonged to either Sounder or Linda—flying regulations and aerodynamics and standard fiction bricks by Clancy, King and Grisham. A cluster at the end could only be hers—*Chop Wood, Carry Water: A Guide to Finding Spiritual Fulfillment in Everyday Life,* Gibran's *The Prophet, The Three Pillars of Zen.* Linda hadn't used all of her years wisely but had been trying to pull things together. Merickel slipped her logbook from atop the bookcase and thumbed the pages. He knew enough pilots to understand how the numbers and sums within would have let Linda fly bigger airplanes to farther away places, but she had wanted to stay here. The bottom shelf held a shiny uncracked bible, some photo albums and her Hoonah High yearbooks. He did not need to open them to know what their portraits looked like each year and where his and her random photos lay—*Friendliest* and *Best Smile* for Linda, *Most Shy* for Merickel.

Despite three decades of history between them, Merickel could not recall ever having been in this cabin Linda had been renting from Deem since the summer before last. The Linda he knew had existed everywhere but here. He hoped this might somehow help him get through his required duties today, but had anyone been there to ask he would have readily admitted to possessing no idea what he was searching for. Merickel supposed he should look for big clues, as any crime committed with bare hands was not one of subtlety and evidence should be equally clumsy. But he saw only the tracks of a couple who cohabitated sporadically until one died and the other disappeared.

Not disappeared, Merickel corrected himself, but simply was not readily available. Sounder could be walking into work right now down in Juneau or, with today's weather, having an oblivious breakfast over at Donna's Restaurant across from the airport. Sounder was thirty, five years the police chief's junior, and in his two years of flying for Westwind maybe twenty words had been exchanged between them. All Merickel knew of him came filtered through Linda. The style of quiet he ran had always struck Merickel less as still waters than that of someone who long ago learned the basic wisdom of not speaking.

A fresh shower streaked the windows, suggesting the methodical coolness this entire process would require. Merickel recalled reading somewhere how composure when no one was looking was a true sign of character. So he sat there drumming a slow beat with his thumb on Linda's kitchen table, knowing full well no one was watching.

☆ ☆ ☆

Joseph Merickel joined the Army through the Delayed Enlistment Program six months before graduating from Hoonah High School. The volatility of the local industries would never suit his nature and he had known himself not ready for college, taking silent credit for such self-appraisal at seventeen. He had just hoped to make out okay and get ahead a little when possible. The next twelve years made Merickel a respected Sergeant First Class and earned him an extension campus degree containing the words *law, technique* and *administration,* though he was now unsure of their actual order. He saw parts of the world he otherwise would not have and came to the conclusion that everybody was basically the same despite different dialects, skin tones and dishes. The MPs showed Merickel what people were capable of, and unlike many who enjoyed the gun on the hip and the armband he never assumed it his job to correct any of that. He merely liked things in order.

Merickel brought his family to Skagway five Augusts ago for just that reason. Crimes were routine and simple. *Busy* meant a softball tournament with rowdy teams down from Whitehorse, a house getting TP'd or a domestic feud fueled by too much beer and too little direct sunlight. The town's seasonal nature spit most kids out after graduation, and those who stayed did so quietly and responsibly. After three years he was invited to replace the existing chief when that man's imbalanced law-keeping finally pissed off a voting majority of the city council. Merickel was in the job less than six months when unsolicited offers from nearby villages began drifting in.

"A little native blood behind the badge goes a long way," he had been told by several selection committees—off the record, of course—and this with Tlingit heritage from only his mother's side. But Merickel had grown up around kids thrown into the big checks of logging and fishing with no legal fun within a hundred miles. Soon they were reeling around on Juneau drugs they had overpaid for, rolling new trucks into the ditch with dealer stickers still on the window. Merickel would not say he was never leaving, but for now was happy with a regular diet of DUIs peppered with fish snagging and fainting tourists.

A peace officer but no detective, he often watched the credits of rented thrillers too embarrassed to ask Jan where the last plot twist was meant to leave him. This mess with poor Linda did not look like a real mystery, but was still more of one than Merickel wanted. No one deserved to die this way, but such things happened to girls in Anchorage who wore satin bar jackets and too much make-up. Women like Linda succumbed to shameless diseases and died in Seattle while the Elks and Eagles held rallies to help pay her medical bills. Or maybe in a car crash that was entirely the other driver's fault. They did not go out like this, and they did not leave old friends behind to connect the dots.

* * *

More freshly removed from procedure manuals than his chief, Lambar had completed his assigned tasks and several others upon Merickel's return. Smug satisfaction rejuvenated his boyish pink face and he offered up a tight note: *Troopers, 1 pm.*

"They were headed out on a call for the rest of the morning, but wanted to speak with the officer in charge." Lambar let a pause state his opinion. "And Canadian customs has no record of Scott Sounder crossing recently. As for Mr. Lester, he hasn't heard from

Scott or Linda in a couple days and figured they were still weathered in up here."

"Johnny doing okay?"

"Fine, I guess. He was upset, of course." Lambar reshuffled his notes, shifting beneath either the question or his own answer. "He's going to try to get in touch with Linda's mother also. I left her a message to call us back. She lives in Littleton now, near Denver."

Nothing on his own desk inspired Merickel to sit down. Any mail appeared bulk or official, and a new PC waited silent and, if possible, smirking. Aside from writing letters and playing with e-mail, he expected little more than improved solitaire skills come winter.

"Any calls from around town?"

Lambar shook his head. "Not so far. Just Jan at about nine-twenty. She wanted to see how you were doing."

Merickel swore he heard a hint of jealousy in Lambar's tone, as if his pure corn-fed soul thought itself somehow more deserving of the sweet domesticity Jan's call implied. A wall clock read 10:44.

"I think I'll cut out now for lunch," Merickel said. "So I can be back when the troopers call."

Lambar said okay and returned a stern gaze to papers both men knew undeserving of such attention. The poor bastard did not know what to do, and Merickel let it slide. If confusion was a crime they would hang side by side.

* * *

An Army buddy of Merickel's—as much of a buddy as the police chief ever had—once said Jan was not the type who inspired a sailor to jump ship, but rather made him notice swells and dread long voyages. Despite the man's ineloquence, Merickel understood. A farmer might call her good breeding stock, though even he recognized such compliments as ill-advised. Merickel just knew that the way she sent him off each morning did not beg a passionate kiss, but simply made him want to return to her that night.

His home's large front window allowed Merickel a view of a televised overbuilt Greek instructor doing leg-lifts somewhere sunny. Jan followed in baggy sweats that hid any results and jumped when she caught her husband staring in from the front steps. Her hug stopped just short of getting his uniform sweaty.

"I'm so sorry, babe," she said. "You don't need this."

He patted her back—damp but no bra. This struck him as more interesting than sexy.

"Any leads?"

Merickel wondered how anyone would discuss murder if not for 1970s detective shows.

"Nothing yet. I suspect Scott Sounder, but we have to find him first."

Jan looked to her onscreen Adonis, smiling through butt clenches under impossible sunlight. "That poor girl."

An ore truck rolled by outside their window, gearing down but still at least ten above the speed limit. Jan placed a hand on his chest as if searching for a pulse.

"I was going to bring you lunch, but I can have it ready in five minutes."

Merickel nodded and let her kiss his forehead like when he left the house bound for exams or evaluations. He joined CNN's news loop and sat enthralled even when Jan placed his grilled cheese and tomato soup next to the chair. The world looked so understandable in the network's quick cycle, with different if not better news mere moments away. Jan emerged with a paper towel after noticing her husband holding buttery fingers above his slacks during sports.

"If you can't make it tonight, that's okay," Jan said. "I won't give details, but the kids will understand."

Merickel sighed. "Oh, I don't see how my staying late will help."

"Do you need anything else before I shower?"

He shook his head and with a quiet pop of her lips Jan started toward the kitchen. She stopped in the doorway with a grasp of the doorsill suggesting unsure footing.

"Is this going to affect your time away?"

Jan reserved the term *vacation* for proper outings with the family to the stores of Juneau or a movie in Whitehorse. Lately, though, she was trying to understand Merickel's need to disappear alone for several days at a time. The habit started during his teenage years in the damp woods around Hoonah, and though he had left it behind when he joined the Army, those sporadic trips were waiting when he returned to Alaska. Maybe someone who so often felt invisible needed to know he could complete the illusion when necessary. Merickel had never made any honest effort to explain, but today Jan's face betrayed real concern.

"I don't know. There's a few days to go yet."

She mouthed "okay" and Merickel soon heard the upstairs shower kick on. He found a list on the kitchen table, begun in his handwriting with *Sterno* and finished in Jan's with *maxi pads.* Merickel took silent pride in never being flustered by purchasing such items. They were necessary and made him feel that much more the family man, comfortable with his mate and her workings. He pocketed the list and left with a warm envy of Jan's noontime shower on a rainy day with no reason to go outside.

* * *

His dash clock read 12:15 and if Merickel knew the troopers he had exactly forty-five minutes to kill. The shopping list held no perishables so he stopped first at the market, where the bubbly checkout girl obviously had not heard. Merickel put the groceries in his Isuzu and walked the two blocks to the Mercantile. Seeing downtown boarded up save for services judged essential for the winter warmed him. He had enjoyed those first couple summers with all the goings-on, but the Outside businesses springing up to support the bigger ships promised by a new dock and Skagway's approaching centennial unsettled him. May waited seven months away but already Merickel viewed the coming summer like a necessary operation he would be glad to see done. Inside the Mercantile a discussion in just that vein was taking place, though a discussion with Art Lowes only meant nodding in agreement while the store owner spoke.

"...and forget zoning. Hell, legitimate shops like mine can't afford space on Broadway. It's all the deep-pocket tourist traps, like you'd find in the islands." Art laughed. "Diamonds, furs, trinkets—shit, I hear we're going to have the Christmas Shoppe two doors down from the St. Nicholas Shop."

The man at the counter had already paid for the hunting vest between them, but Art's corrugated hands held his change hostage. The customer wore a jacket emblazoned with *Kopper King, Whitehorse, YT* and his face betrayed regret at having driven a hundred and eighty kilometers for this. Art took the bell announcing Merickel's arrival like an actor's cue.

"Right, Joe? I thought Christmas came just once a year."

"Apparently it comes every other block now," Merickel said.

"Where's your Sterno hiding these days?"

Art pointed a meaty finger to the store's rear and surrendered the Canuck's change with a deliberateness suggesting some fiscal lesson.

"You need more proof of where things in this town are headed? That man is investigating our first murder in decades."

The customer studied him for hints of blood or the role Sterno played in a homicide investigation. Merickel offered a cracked grin of hello but the man fled north by the time the police chief reached the counter.

"It's probably best not to scare folks like that, Art."

Art seemed to consider a price hike on the spot. He afforded Merickel and the badge more respect than most but enjoyed his trump card of lifetime residency.

"Let him run back to Canada. You suspect that pilot?"

"Kind of early to say."

"He did have that strange look, y'know, when you stared at him hard."

"I suppose most folks would give you a strange look if you stared at them hard, Art."

Merickel threw in some freeze-dried ice cream and rigid energy bars to smooth things over. A Remington 700 with a Leupold Mark IV scope lay beneath the glass case that comprised the counter, drawing a reflexive whistle from Merickel.

"Is that chambered for the .300 Winchester Mag?"

"Sure is." Art made for the lock. "You like? Chuck Hanley just traded her in, practically new. I doubt he even put a full box of shells through her."

Merickel waved him off. "It's just similar to one I got to play around with in the Army."

"What were you doing with this thing in the service?"

"A little precision shooting stuff." Merickel pocketed his change. Three years with the Marksmanship Unit at Fort Benning. Instructor for the Service Rifle Team. Regular groupings at a thousand yards you could cover with your palm. All things Merickel might have said but did not.

"That's right," Art said. "They weren't shooting at real people during your stint, were they?"

Merickel bit his tongue about that possibly being the real test of a peacekeeping force and now found himself looking forward to the troopers' call. Any retort could get ugly and smart people did not make bad blood heading into the winter.

"Thanks, Art. I'll see you around."

* * *

The troopers had already called. Lambar relayed this before the news of a gillnetter missing from the harbor.

"How long?"

"Ten minutes ago. Here's his number."

Merickel eyed the note: *12:43. William Bench, Alaska State Troopers.* A tight underline suggested Lambar had taken as much enjoyment in copying the title as Bench did offering it.

"I actually meant how long has the boat been missing."

"The owner only noticed it gone this morning," Lambar said. "He lives over in Haines but had the boat moored here while he's been home the last couple days. Someone named Dale Crown is giving him a ride up from the harbor."

"Dale Crown?" Merickel restrained today's first legitimate smile. He sat at his desk and took up the phone. Even after a long distance click the line hissed as if all that rain was soaking into the circuits.

"Bench speaking." The voice rang so mechanical Merickel expected an answering machine beep to follow.

"Hello, Joseph Merickel here."

"Thank you for returning my call, Chief Merickel. Sounds like you have a problem up there."

"Yes." Despite eighty miles of water and rock between them Merickel straightened in his chair. "A problem."

"Officer Lambar gave me the pertinent details, and we'll being following up what leads we can down here. I do however need some additional information from you to start my official report. I know you have them but I e-mailed the specific forms that I will need ASAP."

The computer crackled to life when Merickel tapped the plastic mouse. A handful of icons begged to be helpful.

"I'll fill them out this afternoon."

"E-mail isn't completely secure so either fax the forms this evening or hang on to them. I'm flying up tomorrow morning."

Merickel glanced out at the drizzle, making Lambar also look to see what he was missing.

"You're either an optimist or not from here."

"I've been in Juneau two years and Southcentral eight before that with the Major Crimes Unit of the Bureau of Investigation," Bench said. "If the weather does not improve, I'll be arriving on the two p.m. ferry. I will let you know if anything develops on our end and I'm confident you will do the same."

"Will do." Merickel scrawled *ferry* on a Post-it note but wasn't sure why.

"I left my home number as well," Bench said. "I keep reasonable hours but call anytime if necessary. We will talk tomorrow at the latest."

Lambar took the news of Bench's impending arrival with a definite opinion he was either hiding or flaunting. That layer of baby fat might hamper certain ambitions and any hint of this morning's tears would not help.

"Good," he said.

The rustle of oilskins preceded Dale Crown, who was trailed at the door by a thick Norwegian Merickel assumed to be the missing boat's owner. He waved both men through the small half-gate separating the law from the general public.

"Joey Merickel, how the hell are you?"

"Been better, Dale."

Lambar eyed the fishermen. He kept even the girls from the city clerk's office outside the gate when they crossed the hall to borrow staples or copier paper.

Crown's thick hands rose in mock exasperation.

"With these digs I guess you won't be back on the decks anytime soon, huh?"

"Sounds pretty appealing today."

Merickel preferred to think of himself and Dale Crown as counterbalanced weights rather than opposites. The two had served as hands on the *Doreen* out of Hoonah the summer Merickel turned sixteen, his father pulling strings to show the boy what real work was. Crown was a twenty-year-old UW dropout who had bought a one-way ticket north and roamed the docks until the *Doreen*'s skipper took pity. Merickel cashed out his share the first day they could spare him, and Crown had since kept water under his boots as much as possible. The social probabilities of the region's population ensured the two men strayed into each other's orbit every few months, allowing them both the best memories of that summer and some reassurance contained in the fact that the other still existed.

"My boat is missing," the Norwegian said, betraying the slightest accent and even less concern. After all the ocean had thrown his way, a fugitive joyriding his gillnetter appeared a mere inconvenience. "If your man who killed that girl took her, I'd like to start towards finding him."

The notebook Merickel pulled from his desk held only a shopping list for some meal eaten weeks ago.

"Dale, you remember Linda Walker? From Hoonah originally, flew for Johnny Lester?"

Crown shrugged. "I'd probably recognize her. Hell, we might've hooked up somewhere once."

Lambar stood.

"Let's have some respect for the deceased, mister."

Even with his uniform and sidearm Lambar could not help looking soft next to Crown, who was already an easy target for resentment due to the stocky physique and youthful looks his haphazard life should have stolen years ago. Another winter would show Lambar how even the good guys were bastards sometimes. Friends came not by choice but rather time and exposure, and you let things slide or nobody drank coffee with you. Merickel looked to the Norwegian.

"Sir, what's your name?"

"Martin Brobakken. Marty will do."

"And the boat?"

"The *Following Sea*. She runs ten knots at firewall, the galley is only good for storing pots and pans, and she has the nav setup of a Zodiac."

The Norwegian ended with a faithless glance at some cartoon posters imploring kids to just say no. Crown had disappeared to the city clerk's office where he was forcing the receptionist into recognizing him.

"So whoever stole her wasn't going fishing or didn't know his boats all that well," Merickel said.

"Like a pilot." Lambar pulled a graduation gift pen from his breast pocket and drew a bead on the Norwegian. "The boat sounds pretty indistinguishable. How tall was the name printed on the back?"

"Stern," Merickel said, happy that someone present made him feel like a salt. The Norwegian held two cracked fingers about six inches apart. Lambar tapped his pen but wrote nothing.

"Small font. And under the name it says Haines, right?"

The Norwegian surrendered the minimum expression necessary to imply *of course*. Lambar reclined—no more questions.

"An unremarkable boat with small print reading Haines when the murder took place here. A smart choice for someone on the run."

The Norwegian looked to Merickel, whose thumb traced a slow deliberate waltz on his desk's laminate surface.

"How long had she been docked here?" Merickel said.

"Since late on Monday. I'd let a friend use her some for the dog run and he came up here to clean her because there was no space down in Haines. My oldest just ran me over this morning so as to pick her up, and that's when we found her gone."

"And your friend, he no doubt left her near the bottom of the ramp?"

The Norwegian nodded.

"At the pumps with plenty of fuel?"

"Yep."

"First boat there. Lots of gas."

Lambar studied the heavy pen when Merickel looked his way. The young man would learn that those who committed simple impulsive acts rarely summoned logic in the aftermath. After Lambar took down the remaining details Merickel saw the Norwegian to the door. The man acknowledged without speaking the police chief's promise to contact the Coast Guard and tacked out to Crown's borrowed rig with the plodding gait of someone who was no highliner and did not need such annoyances heading into the off-season.

Merickel pulled Crown from the clerk's office.

"What brings you so far north?"

"Just finishing the dog run on the Chilkat," Crown said. "Like Marty probably told you, Haines's grid is booked all week and my screws look like cauliflower. I came up yesterday to scrape the belly before the winter. High tide is around three so I've got time for a beer."

Lambar lay in Merickel's peripherals, head down but listening.

"Not the best time, Dale. I still have to talk with the local paper, and the kids have a school thing tonight."

Crown's easy nod said the dock would offer plenty of alternatives.

"Good enough. I'm heading to Juneau in the morning, so if I don't see you, have a good winter." Crown craned to see Lambar. "You too, Barney Fife."

With Crown gone Merickel gave Lambar a *What can you do?* look but remained in the hall among the literature for passport renewal and city council meeting minutes. The rain had picked up.

"What can you do?" His own words came so quiet Merickel was unsure afterwards if they were merely a thought.

⁂

Skagway's last entertainment of the moving variety had come three years earlier, a summer carnival boasting a big top the south wind almost carried away and the town's first elephant. People snatched up five-dollar tickets and sat through clumsy jugglers and a pasty contortionist to watch the beast forego its regular act and rear up for a two-minute fire-hydrant piss. This set the standard for travelling shows very high.

Hope for similar unplanned amusement drew people to what a school flyer called *One Magical Evening*. A worn Laidlaw school bus with Northwest Territories plates and windows blacked out by trash bags skulked behind the gym, and Jan reported seeing a less than mystical crew unloading crates. But tonight was a benefit and younger students were allowed to participate, Joe Merickel Junior included.

"Ask if they can make you disappear," Merickel said as the boy, in all black with a fake moustache, left for rehearsal with his sister in tow. Her parting glance promised she would look into the matter.

The reason for the children's involvement became apparent after the curtain rose. The magic was subpar, the beautiful assistant strung out or recently recovered, and most would have left in short order had their kids not been hostages. Merickel stepped out when a girl was levitated with a click audible over the background music. Too many eyes in the passing shadows pleaded for morbid or reassuring details, and those that didn't promised they would be sleeping with a loaded firearm no more than an arm's reach away.

Outside low clouds absorbed an orange glow from the city lights and the diehard smokers held court beneath an overhang. Merickel acknowledged them with a tight nod before noticing Calhoun among their ranks.

"Evening, Chief Joseph."

The words came from the flare of an inhaling cigarette, beyond which lay lips begging to say *Not on my watch.*

"How you doing, Jeff?"

"All right, considering. What's the latest?"

"We're working on things. The troopers get here tomorrow."

"Grubbs?" Calhoun said. "I worked with him a few times."

"Some fellow named Bench." The hand Merickel extended out from the doorway's shelter soaked over in seconds.

"Well, help's here if you need it."

Calhoun turned back to his cabal. Despite the former police chief's six feet of height, relaxed-fit denims, and layer of hairy flab riding real muscle, Merickel recognized in the shadows the outline of a simple bully. The MP ranks had held plenty like him and they could handle most enforcement capacities just fine. But Merickel had spent three winters watching Calhoun's law sway around the variables of mood, relation to those involved, and any audience he hoped to impress. Keeping order required a certain relativity, but also demanded a constant.

"Thanks, Jeff."

Back inside the hallway bass-heavy music pulsed through the walls, suggesting a welcome finale. Merickel paused at the trophy case to review an athletic history he already knew by heart. The doors to the multi-purpose room clicked out of his sight like a cocking pistol. Jan's look of concern dropped the instant she saw him.

"The kids are coming on soon."

Merickel fell in behind, studying his wife's generously-cut black jeans and nondescript sweater. Jan's hips sported honest fat and her shoulders could belong to a rancher's daughter raised on daily morning labor. Even if the urge she gave rise to was not visceral, he took comfort from his interest in returning to those hips and shoulders. This body cared more for others than itself. Not like Linda. She had inspired emotion, good and bad. Maybe if she had been chunkier or a little more plain. Who knew?

* * *

The blinking answering machine light made Merickel anxious, but he waited until Jan had the kids down for the night to retrieve the message.

A beep, then: "Joe, Johnny here. A goddamn shame, this whole mess. Listen..." A static hesitation. "We medevaced some sorry-ass out of Excursion with a broken arm late today, and rumor is Scott was involved. Call me whenever you get in."

Merickel took up the thin phonebook containing the numbers for all of Southeast's smaller towns and villages. Important contacts lay handwritten inside the front cover, Johnny Lester's fourth from the top. He chose the old rotary phone in the back porch, where the furnace muffled conversation and insinuated a desire for privacy.

The sound of an overly-loud TV answered and Merickel felt a stab of pity. Johnny's daughters were both grown and flown south and lately the man's jokes about he and the old lady rang a little too true to be funny anymore.

"Johnny, it's Joe. Hey, I apologize for having Lambar call, I should've done it myself."

"Don't worry about it, kid. These things screw you up."

Merickel nodded to nobody but himself. "How you holding up?"

"Okay, considering everything," Johnny said. "Losing two good pilots hurts, even if we've barely spun a prop since Monday. And, Jesus, of all people to go... but I don't have to tell you that." His pause suggested a beer or something harder. "You get my message about the guy with the broken arm?"

"Yeah." Merickel reviewed last year's calendar on the back door, all those days and appointments dead and buried. "Yeah I did."

"The guy claimed he fell," Johnny said. "But he looked pretty worked over."

"Huh." Merickel found himself writing XIP—the shipping code for Excursion Inlet Packing—in pencil on a paper scrap before scratching the letters out.

"Anyway, the troopers were by earlier today to ask about Scott and Linda, but I haven't called them back with this," Johnny said. "Still, it might be worth checking into if you can get down this way."

"Yeah, I think you're right." Merickel looked out at heavy rain only visible streaking through the streetlight's halo. "Let me check some things and I'll be in touch tomorrow, okay?"

"Good enough. Hang in there, sheriff."

Merickel went into the kitchen for some cold two percent, off the barge Tuesday but still only three good days left. The water heater told him Jan was showering. He wanted to keep refilling his glass and sit up wondering about nothing more important than when this rain would let up. He wanted to restore the peace, and he wanted Linda to be alive again. He wanted do the right thing, and wanted the right thing to be what was rattling around in his head like the small stones inside that rock polisher he had as a kid. He wanted to fall asleep knowing what would happen tomorrow. Twenty-four ounces later, he did.

* * *

Five-thirty came as Merickel hoped—thick drops tapped the panes and the same wet glowing cones hung beneath the streetlights.

He always woke before his alarm clock but allowed the tired KHNS DJ a minute before silencing the radio. Most mornings he strolled the house and watched CNN muted over cold cereal, opting to stand atop the heating vent and study the street outside when lows dropped into the twenties. Today the TV stayed dormant while Merickel filled a duffel with three days worth of clothes from the laundry and placed the bag on the porch. He roused Jan thirty minutes before her usual time and gave her a sparse rundown. The early hour and fatigue combined for a simple understanding smile. He kissed her and left, confident that no observer could claim his actions had been calculated rather than thrown together on impulse.

Crown's *Great Notion* was off the harbor's grid and tied near the pumps, empty but unlocked. A quick search of downtown would likely find the fisherman breakfasting at the Sweet Tooth or Prospector, but Merickel did not want a coffee klatch public record showing that he sought Crown out. He tore a page from a yellow pad containing some doodles and Juneau phone numbers and left his note on the skipper's seat.

Lambar often preceded his chief to the office, but last night was the first volleyball session without Linda, who, although short, had brought real hustle. If Merickel hadn't suspected his junior officer would mourn with extra sleep he would have foregone the stop at city hall. Under minimal lighting he began a handwritten outline of tasks and contact numbers and had barely finished when the phone rang at six-fifty. He relaxed upon recognizing the tinfoil connection of the harbormaster phone.

"Joe, it's Crown. You still need a ride?"

Merickel shut off his desk lamp and stood.

"Yeah. I'm on foot, so maybe fifteen minutes?"

"I'll have her warmed up and waiting."

Merickel considered using the rear exit, but thought better and walked without reservation down the front steps onto a damp street belonging only to him.

* * *

Their smooth ride out of the bay was the first upside Merickel had seen to this stretch of stable wet weather. October was capable of much rougher stuff, and several times Crown muttered asides about their good fortune and taking calm seas over good visibility any day in the Big Lynn. Aside from pockmarks of rain, the glassy surface faded around them into a grey mist and Taiya Inlet revealed only a few hundred feet of its steep walls off each rail. One of Crown's gizmos on the dash glowed with a blocky moving map, at the screen's center an innocent square that Merickel assumed to be the *Great Notion*. Crown beamed like a proud father over his collection of gadgets, alien visitors on the beaten wood console.

"You ever screw around with this GPS stuff, Joe?"

Merickel sat aft in the wheelhouse sipping black coffee. "Just a little of the early stuff, on military training exercises."

Crown fiddled with the scale knob. "Pretty breakthrough shit. Instead of wandering around looking for shoreline, it tells you exactly where you are. Even if you don't like where you are, at least you know."

The Katzehin River flats drifted by like an anxious dream in the fog. Crown apologized for cancelling his satellite TV prematurely and worked on picking up the Juneau AM station as a distant consolation prize.

"So, does this have anything to do with that dead girl's boyfriend?" Crown looked pleased with himself for having shown forty-five minutes of restraint, during which time they had done little more than volley around old names that inspired headshakes, anecdotes or knowing chuckles.

"He tops the list, between you and me and the door." Merickel put his coffee down. "You sticking around Juneau long?"

Crown eyed the bow. "Who knows? I need to get her winterized and wait for some checks to clear. Then maybe I'll go kick around Seattle for a month or so, see what happens."

Visits with Crown always reminded Merickel why he had forgone a life of boats and fish and the inherently uncertain waters the two shared. But people doing things they should not do—there was a career with consistency upon which you could build a schedule.

Merickel excused himself below after Seduction Point passed off the starboard rail as nothing more than a ghost story and the AM radio began offering intermittent company. Crown's bed was made but playing host to music CDs and unlaundered Levis. Merickel moved the jeans and fought his instinct to match the misaligned CDs with their correct cases. Last night's sleep had been like running in sand, and now he was at least moving toward something. Jan had found him a dog-eared block of Stephen Coonts at the library paperback exchange and he took comfort in the thriller's promise to put him out, while Crown and his computers kept them off the rocks and clear of a northbound ferry somewhere out on the Lynn Canal carrying a trooper named Bench.

* * *

The slap of swells just inches from his head woke Merickel. In the wheelhouse Crown sat absorbed listening to Problem Corner on KINY, where someone had a small boat trailer for sale but would consider swapping for a decent truck winch. They were inside Mab Island, Crown explained, a northerly around Berners Bay having started the chop but also gained them several knots. That same wind forced the clouds a couple thousand feet up the green mountains, leaving tenuous wisps in the treetops.

The *Great Notion* pulled into Auke Bay harbor under a steady parade of piston planes, freshly-released off the Juneau airport. Crown had no immediate plans for the beaten Ford Bronco he kept at the top of the ramp, and after tying lines Merickel left with a promise to return the vehicle before dark. The Bronco's passenger window was half open and five days worth of rain had puddled on the seat. A scattering of empties hinted that the lawman would not have approved of her last outing. He tossed the cans in a dumpster and headed toward the airport with the Bronco blowing a defeated version of heat.

Waiting passengers swarmed around the terminal's taxidermied animals now permanently fixed with waxy snarls and bared claws. A teenage girl sat smirking at her *People* magazine behind the Westwind Airways counter, which was surprisingly free of patrons, baggage and other maladies. When Merickel inquired about Johnny, she lowered the magazine only enough to ensure he was not one of *The 50 Most Beautiful People of 1994*.

"He's on a run out to Tenakee. Should be back by around four, maybe four-thirty."

Merickel tapped the counter. "Could you tell him Joe stopped by and I'll try back a little later?"

"Sure," she said. "But if the weather drops there's no guarantee he'll get back tonight."

He offered a smile absolving her of any responsibility and left to take a room at the nearby Travelodge, thumbing the department credit card momentarily but finally paying with his own. Then off to Costco, where the unsmiling fence of Lemon Creek Correctional Center stared over the parking lot trees. Merickel filled his big cart with Listerine, cereal, muffins and pattern-free toilet paper, adding matching winter coats for the kids and a case of Budweiser for Crown on the way to the register. Dropping his goods at the Skagway Air Service counter he was informed that the flyable conditions had not reached home yet and his boxes lay behind three days of backlog.

A group of pilots in various air taxi jackets hung near the Westwind counter. After days of drinking coffee and staring out at the weather they looked reenergized by the afternoon's activity. The girl saw Merickel approaching and gestured toward an open door behind her. He paused passing across the baggage scale—one hundred seventy-four, within five pounds of all his Army physicals.

Johnny Lester began a single-plane service twenty-five years ago and operated under the Westwind name three summers before people called him anything but "that big guy with the red DeHavilland." Even back then he was an anachronism, forgoing rigid schedules to look for whales and passing low over town so you could see your house from a hundred feet up. Merickel went to work for Johnny in Hoonah after his summer on the *Doreen*, showing up on weekends and after school to sell tickets, heft bags and calculate the weight and balance manifests. He had enjoyed the simple straightforward tasks and learning exactly what numbers would and would not fly. Johnny had jammed an extra two hundred dollars into their handshake when Merickel left for basic training and guaranteed him a lifetime of free flights home.

Now Westwind had twelve airplanes—straight floats, amphibs and fixed gear—that went "Any place worth going and a few that aren't." So boasted the air service's newest color brochure, a big step for someone whose first attempt at advertising was carving his name and number near all the harbor payphones between Wrangell and Pelican. The Johnny that Merickel remembered hung in photos and yellowing newspaper clippings around the office. Behind his desk sat a man who had raised two kids in the dirty snow of Juneau and spent too many lousy afternoons waiting for all his airplanes to return. His barrel-like bulk sagged more and showed some mileage, but he looked invigorated by today's lifting clouds. Johnny pushed aside his flight bag to clear a seat.

"C'mon in, Joe. I thought the canal was still down."

"I caught a ride on Dale Crown's boat. Remember him?"

Johnny gave a loose affirmation and gestured out to his wet Cessnas, their cowlings steaming from recent use.

"Sorry I missed you earlier. The weather's got us behind so when things broke open I had to help out."

"You doing okay? Big picture?"

Johnny huffed like a low tire that would get the driver home but not much farther.

"The girls tell me they're good, and Margie hasn't changed the locks yet. We'll see what winter brings. How about on your end?"

"Status quo, I guess, right up until yesterday morning." Merickel pulled a pad and pen from his coat pocket. "So what's the deal with this Excursion fellow?"

"One of my guys brought him in late yesterday, said he fell down the stairs." Johnny fumbled with an errant headset cord. "There aren't enough stairs in the whole damn inlet to do someone over like that. Everyone out at the cannery was pretty tight-lipped, but my pilot got the idea that Scott might be involved."

Merickel wrote *stairs* on his pad and circled the word.

"The guy's an equipment tech out there," Johnny said. "Has a wife and kids in Angoon. We bring him back and forth occasionally when he comes into Juneau to get loaded up. I dropped him at Bartlett hospital last night." He made a quick search for a note. "Dan Gilbert. Anything?"

Merickel shook his head. The phone Johnny pushed his way bore a snapshot of a now heavier but still smiling Margie taped to the keypad. Maybe hope remained.

A clinical voice answered and apologized that they could not give out patient information over the phone. She peeped "okay" when Merickel volunteered his title and after a brief hold said Gilbert had checked out earlier that afternoon. He thanked her and hung up.

"He's gone."

Johnny stood and signaled for Merickel to follow. For a big man he moved swiftly through the airport's familiar territory and had the answer he wanted by the time Merickel reached the L.A.B. Flying Service counter. Dan Gilbert had returned to Excursion Inlet on L.A.B.'s first flight today after the weather lifted. Johnny snatched the next day's schedule before his *People*-loving employee could even look up and headed to his office, where he studied the papers until Merickel felt obligated to speak.

"What about Scott?"

Johnny's look was that of a man who could not lie but had hoped the question wouldn't come up.

"Joe, I've never worried about him hurting anyone in my airplanes," he said. "But otherwise I give Scott wide berth."

"I don't follow."

"We both know a lot of guys push it out there. Nothing crazy, just getting the job done." Johnny contemplated his desktop as if the surface held more than scrawled part numbers and coffee rings. "But Scott flies right by the numbers and isn't afraid to report perfectly workable weather as below minimums or turn someone in for being out when they shouldn't be. If anyone says anything he throws regs back at them like scripture."

Merickel watched a young Westwind pilot leading four passengers out to his plane. "So he isn't making friends, but that's not wrong, is it?"

Johnny crossed his arms. "Hey, I'd rather have live passengers in here bitching about turning back than dead ones over on Admiralty Island."

Both men averted their gaze out of respect for those who supplied the ready example—1987, a Westwind 207 with six aboard into the side of Mt. Robert Barron. The FAA settled on pilot error and insurance settlements pushed Johnny's retirement back at least three years.

"Scott's good at keeping things in between the lines in the air," Johnny said. "But we both know life isn't that way all the time."

"Do any of the other guys know him better?"

Johnny fidgeted with a pen boasting the fastest and best fuel service in Ketchikan. Big words for a pen.

"He mostly keeps to himself. Scott's affable enough, but it's like he's always... thinking. Noticing little things that are wrong."

"What's his background?"

"Military, actually. Air Force." Johnny said this in the vein of so many civilians who assumed the service branches interchangeable, as if Merickel and Sounder shared a pew at church.

"And he came to fly for you?" Merickel smiled. "No offense."

Johnny grinned. "Well, kinda military. He did the Academy in Springs but wasn't quite up to snuff and washed out at the tail end of flight training. The Air Force kept him on in a non-flying position for a while, but after Desert Storm they started cutting back. They offered him a chance to get out early with an honorable discharge, so he took it. All that still weighs pretty heavy on him, and he practically apologized for it during his interview."

Merickel felt for Sounder, an apparent lover of numbers and tolerances betrayed by his beloved. "I can think of worse albatrosses."

"Yeah, but that's Scott," Johnny said. "I get the feeling he lets all this little stuff build up, and maybe Linda was just there when everything popped loose. I always wondered what she saw in him."

During Merickel's eleventh year Linda had taken in a injured marten she found at the dump. She hid the animal in a cardboard box in her mom's garage, where it hissed at offers of food but eventually ate. A week later Linda lifted her shirt to show Merickel a white belly still swollen from the rabies shots necessitated by the bite on her hand. The marten had crapped all over the garage and fled out an open window while she held fresh puncture wounds so deep they did not even bleed.

"I guess she just saw the best in people."

Johnny released a sigh to shake off the entire day and retook his schedule.

"You up for a trip to Excursion tomorrow around ten?" he said. "I'm flying the run through Icy Strait myself, maybe we can poke around a little."

"I'll be there." Merickel stood. "I'm at the Travelodge if anything changes."

Johnny rose, patting his paunch out of habit to clear anything that might have fallen there.

"I'd have you over, Joe, but I'm going to be here late, and things..." Merickel took this to mean Johnny did not expect a warm plate tonight and two would be a real stretch.

"That's okay, Johnny. I haven't been in the big city in a while, so I'm due some fast food. I'll see you tomorrow morning."

Johnny extended his big paw. "In the morning then."

* * *

Crown was not aboard the *Great Notion*, likely shanghaied by dockmates and promises of the last shared drink or pretty girls until spring. Merickel left the Bronco key and Budweiser in the skipper's chair and entertained thoughts of walking the three miles back to the Travelodge, but a fog with aspirations hung in the trees. He found a payphone outside the nearby liquor store and decided it prudent to call a cab before his office. A Coors Light clock read four fifty-six and the register girl inside eyed him skeptically for not purchasing anything.

"Skagway Police Department, Lambar."

"It's Joseph."

"Hello, *Joe*." Lambar played his name like a curveball, right into the glove of Trooper Bench no doubt sitting nearby. "We've been waiting for your call."

"I got in later than expected. Any planes today?"

"I haven't heard any," Lambar said. "Mr. Bench came on the ferry. He wants to speak with you."

"I figured."

The sound of a palm filled the receiver, then:

"Chief Merickel."

"Hello again, Mr. Bench."

"Apparently we missed each other. Perhaps I wasn't clear with my itinerary."

Merickel wondered how long it had taken Bench to pull the "sirs" off even his simplest responses.

"You were. My coming to Juneau was sort of a last minute thing this morning, and I didn't want to wake you."

"For future reference, I check my work voicemail at the top of every hour from seven a.m. to eight p.m. And your note..." Merickel saw the trooper, hat still on and having reviewed his simple note a hundred times already, or at least at the top of every hour. "It was not very specific."

"Yeah, a friend of mine medevaced someone in from Excursion Inlet, and Scott Sounder may be involved."

"A friend of yours?"

"Johnny Lester, the owner of Westwind."

"Why didn't Mr. Lester call us?"

Merickel searched for his cab. "We go way back and it is, after all, just speculation. I'm meeting with the man from Excursion tomorrow. Dan Gilbert is the name."

"Dan...Gilbert." Merickel envisioned Bench's notepad, a heavy spiral number void of frayed edges and doodles, serviced by a pen that emitted a heavy click when called to duty. "Well, this is a little unorthodox, but I have a few tasks up here, so you can go ahead with Gilbert. Perhaps you would like Trooper Grubbs from my office to come along."

A beaten station wagon bearing a Capitol Cab logo crawled along the dock road. Merickel waved the car over and the driver dropped into park with a nonchalance saying his meter was running.

"I appreciate the offer, Mr. Bench, but this Gilbert doesn't sound like someone who would respond real well to a trooper."

Over the hissing line he felt Bench estimating the worth of such a person.

"If this is solid, it won't matter if he likes troopers or not," Bench said. "I'll expect updates and a report as soon as you are done tomorrow. And going forward, Chief Merickel, we need to make sure we communicate better."

This begged a response and Merickel scrambled for the minimum. "I understand."

Glacier Highway hissed by under the cab's tires and Merickel wondered why he had not told Bench that he would be flying out to Excursion Inlet rather than visiting Gilbert at the hospital. He looked at the number Bench had given for Trooper Grubbs once more before burying the note behind money he did not plan to spend.

At the Travelodge he laid out tomorrow's clothes and called Jan. She spoke of the continued rain, the wake of disappointment trailing the magic show, and used her limited nautical vocabulary to ask about the voyage down. She did not inquire about his return, but before hanging up he hinted tomorrow evening, Sunday at the latest.

A peek outside revealed the tired lights of an adjacent bar, cars sizzling through standing water, and mist suggesting multiple layers. When Merickel left he double-checked the door lock and slipped his wallet into the front pocket of his jeans. Like so many from the surrounding villages, he grew up hearing how Juneau kids took speed and people were assaulted in broad daylight and several other societal side effects associated with stoplights and buildings taller than two stories. The Army had taken Merickel more than a few places in this world, but walking to McDonald's he could not help revisiting the dull warm fear of being a dumb out-of-town kid whose biggest worry was not being of this place.

* * *

For first-time travelers flying from Juneau to Gustavus, the isolated buildings of Excursion Inlet came as a false summit. Gustavus lay only five miles further to the west, but no roads connected that community with the inlet cutting north into the Chilkat Mountains like a neglected fracture that would never properly heal. A few private summer cabins crawled up the bay's far edges, but when most folks said Excursion they meant the cannery.

The canning facility had been Merickel's first job outside Hoonah. His father sent him the twenty miles across Icy Strait at fifteen, the summer before he sailed on the *Doreen*. Merickel despised the place from day one and though his dad always said he was free to come home, this disclaimer came in the tone parents adopt when inviting failure for use as future firepower. He had muscled through his ten-week contract, spending any free time on the surrounding trails or bunked out, and visited home only for the Fourth of July and one other time at his mother's urging. That summer remained one of the wettest on record and though at the time Merickel had bought his old man's line about building character, he now wondered what kind of character resulted from a person doing something they hated.

The dimensions of Icy Strait felt familiar but tighter than Merickel remembered as Johnny skimmed a low stratus layer over Point Couverden. His summer on the *Doreen* had cemented the area's basic navigation points shared by pilots and sailors with the effective glue of dire weather—high winds rounding Point Augusta, six foot swells off Homeshore, someone swamping near Point Retreat. The public schools could benefit by infusing a little visceral terror when teaching geography.

Only after passing beyond a patchwork of clear-cut foothills and descending into the inlet did Merickel remember fall was upon them. The leaves hummed an angry orange and waited for a proper north wind to send them into the bay. Johnny overflew the cannery before slicing the glassy water with the DeHavilland Beaver's floats. The season over, they had the dock to themselves. A heavyset man stood atop the ramp, lobbing marble-sized stones at a squadron of gulls who circled the clear waters out of optimism and habit, their four-month feast of entrails now cut off. Only after the lines were tied up did he acknowledge his visitors.

"Summer must be over," the man said. "If they let you out among the public."

Johnny's grin accepted the requisite scrap of truth riding on the back of everything funny. Their handshake resembled a bundle of cables.

"Tyrone, this is Joe Merickel, Chief of Police in Skagway. He's here to see Dan Gilbert." Johnny turned to Merickel. "Tyrone lives up the inlet and works as a caretaker during the off-season."

Tyrone offered no hand so Merickel gave his reflexive compact greeting.

"Joe grew up over in Hoonah and even worked a summer here way back when," Johnny added. If this was meant to boost Merickel's credibility, it did not take.

"You going to arrest the stairs?" Tyrone's chuckle pleaded for support. "Talk to the dumpster. Or the pump shack. They saw the whole thing."

"Just a few questions."

Johnny came to Merickel's rescue. "If I hear right, those same stairs also did Linda in."

Tyrone grimaced. Another couple weeks and he would be alone with the gulls.

"I think he's packing up at the bunkhouse." Tyrone looked north, maybe sending a telepathic warning to Gilbert. "He's expecting a friend's boat to take him home to Angoon any time now."

Merickel thanked him and looked to Johnny.

"You go ahead," Johnny said. "I'm going to visit, see what there is for me to pick up."

"Just a couple boxes of clothes the workers left behind," Tyrone said. "Donate them to the Glory Hole in town for all I care."

Merickel followed a forklift alley between buildings and caged walls into an open lot littered with rusted organs of obsolete machinery too heavy to dispose of properly. Excursion Inlet existed in his memory as a collection of noises—gruff pneumatics, idling boats and impatient backup beepers—and even this morning the dormant facility hummed with a latent energy, ready to leap to life and tangle a person in her workings. He passed into a clearing where the older kids used to drink and hold bonfires, the fire pit and halo of empties confirming the tradition continued. A cement barrier held some young Romeo's spray-paint proclamation, and Merickel wished their northern romance luck down south, knowing too well how some loves existed only in specific regions and during certain times of year.

A door with loose glass panes slammed beyond a stand of trees. A few quick steps through knee-deep brush put Merickel back on the road, where Dan Gilbert was walking toward him. If this was his escape attempt, it was a pathetic one. A duffel rivaling his own torso hung from Gilbert's good shoulder while a slung left arm made any movements arthritic. Well into his thirties, the man had probably kept the same hat and haircut since high school and his black eye did not look like a precedent. Merickel thought of a dog hunched over a bone with no intention of chewing, just growling.

"Dan Gilbert?"

A stranger who knew his name—a definite red flag.

"Yeah?"

"Joseph Merickel, Chief of Police from Skagway."

Gilbert's good eye tried not to squint.

"You got a minute?" Merickel said.

"Shit, man." Gilbert's face and voice cracked in unison. "I didn't know being clumsy was illegal."

"It isn't. Let me help you with your stuff."

Gilbert lacked the pride to refuse and surrendered his duffel with a grunt to prove the help warranted. Gravel under their boots was the only sound until Merickel spoke.

"Must be good friends to come from Angoon to pick you up."

Gilbert coughed. "They've been up at the dog salmon run in Haines. It's on their way home."

"And your family is in Angoon?"

"A wife and two girls." Gilbert put this forth like a plea for leniency.

"Did you ever play basketball against Hoonah in high school?" Merickel said. "That's where I'm from originally. I know we were in the same conference."

"I didn't grow up in Angoon," Gilbert said. "We're just there because of my wife's folks. We want to get the hell out, but . . . anyway, I never did sports."

"Me neither," Merickel said. "So you knew Linda Walker?"

"I flew in with her a couple times." He cleared his nose and spit into the nearby grass. "I heard about her dying and all."

"Y'know, Mr. Gilbert, getting beat up isn't illegal either."

Merickel could not tell if this came as a revelation to the man.

"I don't see what you're getting at."

"I think Scott Sounder did this to you," Merickel said. "That's as simple as I can put it."

Gilbert's laugh cracked like dry branches underfoot.

"If that was the case, why didn't he just kill me too?"

Despite his bravado, this question did not sound rhetorical.

"I was hoping we could try to figure that out."

The empty north dock left the shore as wood and ended thirty feet out in a float of cement and steel. The handrails bore carved vessel names and miscalculated amorous equations. Dan Gilbert's boat had yet to come in and he offered no word of thanks when Merickel set his bag down.

"Talk if you want, but when they get here I'm gone."

"Fair enough." Merickel gave the empty inlet another glance. "How well did you and Linda know each other?"

Gilbert brought a fidgety hand to his mouth, realizing at the last minute he had no cigarette. "People been talking?"

Merickel's blood flushed like locking his keys in the car a hundred times over. "They tend to do that."

"Fuckers." Gilbert spat and watched the phlegm spread like a jellyfish on the water. "People shouldn't talk about stuff they don't know shit about."

"That wouldn't leave much for conversation."

"You said it." Gilbert looked south. "We were different, y'know. Linda was more uptown, and me..."

Gilbert seemed to search for a good way to admit to being a

fuckup who'd had a dozen second chances, or maybe he had not come to realize this yet. Merickel could respect the effort such a ruse took on an overcast October morning waiting for friends who may or may not show.

"We were different," Gilbert said again before mumbling through an ambiguous tale that began with small talk on flights back and forth to Juneau, then picnics of chips and Cokes up at Neva Lake when Linda had a little extra time at the cannery.

"She wasn't like the others," Gilbert said. "All the girls here either look like lingcods or are stuck-up bitches. But Linda . . . she listened, y'know?"

Merickel said he did know. Linda had always listened—listened and then asked questions that showed she had been paying attention, and when you answered she looked at you in a way that made you just keep answering and answering, because you knew those eyes were seeing everything so you might as well spill it all. When low clouds and mist had grounded her in Excursion for a night, Gilbert volunteered his spare bunk. Merickel could not imagine a bed in the cannery worthy of Linda, not even those reserved for visiting investor bigwigs.

"So you and her . . . ?"

Had Gilbert's locker-room grin broken a fraction more Merickel would have pushed the one-armed bastard backwards into the inlet.

"Gentlemen don't kiss and tell."

Merickel pocketed his hands to hide their shaking.

"You and I can do this here, Mr. Gilbert, or the troopers can do it in Juneau."

Gilbert crushed an empty off-brand soda can that lay near his foot and sent the carcass into the water.

"Nothing happened, man. Fucking happy now?"

Merickel allowed himself a stabilizing breath. "Come again?"

"Nothing happened. Not even making out. We just talked." Gilbert appeared worried that he might be cited for cowardice. "But it wasn't so far out there, man, if I had tried. So people talked and I let them. What's the harm, right?"

Merickel scrutinized Gilbert's busted arm and the smaller man pulled away.

"Did you know Scott Sounder before this?"

"A little, but he didn't fly in here often. Linda said he liked regular runs with fixed schedules." The man cradled his slung wing with a fondness his children likely would not recognize. "He suckered me coming out of the mess hall. If I'd had a second to get ready..."

Merickel's face told Gilbert he need not bother continuing.

"Did he say anything?"

Gilbert dug cigarettes out from his bag. "Some stupid shit about me deserving this. The guy's a fucking nut job, right?"

"So you told everyone you fell down the stairs." The voice in Merickel's throat finally felt like his own.

"I hadn't heard about Linda and just didn't want my wife finding out. And I wanted to keep the cops out of it."

"Liking someone's girl isn't a crime," Merickel said. "Just bad business."

"Amen to that." Gilbert lit a cigarette he obviously thought earned. The sureness of his first drag assured Merickel that Gilbert had also earned what Sounder gave him.

"How did you feel when you heard Linda was dead?"

The words were a punch Merickel should have pulled but he enjoyed Gilbert's expression of shock, despite its looking worn from overuse.

"What the fuck do you think? It sucks. I felt bad."

Merickel wondered whether Gilbert's emotional scale or just his vocabulary limited the response. He wanted to grasp the man's shoulders, good and bad, and send him down below that lightless surface where he belonged. Both men turned at a chugging sound. From beyond the cannery an abused gillnetter slipped into view.

"How old are your girls, Mr. Gilbert?"

Smoke curled around the man's upper lip. "Four and six."

"And your wife's number is in the Angoon book?"

Gilbert stood up yet looked smaller. "You better not talk to her before I get home."

The threat rang so hollow the approaching boat's engine swallowed the words at near idle. Merickel started up the ramp.

"I suspect nothing I could tell her would come as much of a surprise." Merickel usually had little use for dramatic wordplay, and it figured the one time things worked to his liking the lone witness was a bottom feeder like Dan Gilbert. "Thank you for your time."

The gillnetter was motoring out of the inlet by the time Merickel reached the cannery office. He imagined Gilbert in the wheelhouse, drinking his friend's beer and putting as much of a spin on their run-in as one and a half arms allowed. He felt no desire to supply a counterpoint. If those aboard knew Dan Gilbert well enough to pick him up, they knew how to take his tale.

The equal masses of Johnny and Tyrone sat across from each other in the cafeteria. The room was sterilized for the winter, the only sign of spice a lazy susan on the table between them hosting a United Nations of condiments. Tyrone spun the accessory slowly and continued a discourse about local kids not having the work ethic to slime fish anymore so they brought up the Mexicans and Filipinos and gave them boning knives and suddenly the bunkhouses were full of international incidents. He was stocking up on conversation for the off-season and surrendered only a sidelong glance at the approaching police chief.

"Get your man?"

"I got what I needed."

"Justice prevails again, huh?"

Merickel remained just long enough to make eye contact with Johnny.

"I'll be out here."

The gulls still circled ten minutes later when Johnny and Merickel untied the Beaver's lines. Tyrone had not accompanied them to the dock, citing pressing business in the big freezer.

"He's not a bad guy," Johnny said. "I guess being pissy just makes some people feel like they stand for something."

Merickel didn't understand but agreed anyway.

* * *

Johnny asked no questions about Dan Gilbert. The five-minute flight from Excursion Inlet to Gustavus barely allowed him time enough to drop the amphib wheels for the runway, and fuel burn alone made their cargo of two crates of bananas a financial loss. This was in no way helped by using the DeHavilland—though a staple of Southeast aviation, the plane's ancient radial engine and associated maintenance costs all but begged to be replaced by a newer Cessna Caravan or 206. But Johnny had instituted this bi-weekly milk run through Icy Strait decades ago, often launching with no definite promise of freight or passengers at any of the stops, and some losing propositions died hard. Usually resulting in little more than dockside socializing and wasted avgas, the venture's lack of economic sense would make anyone with business schooling cringe. Still, the world at times demanded a person go through the motions, even when they knew their actions would come to nothing.

The scattershot components of Gustavus spread themselves across a wide flood plain at the mouth of Glacier Bay, disappearing among the taller trees as Johnny descended to the airstrip. Merickel had long harbored an admiration for the town's four hundred reclusive inhabitants. No dominant industry existed to draw people in and a lack of state ferry service meant no curious vagabonds wandering ashore—residency was an educated choice. An expansive airport left over from World War II comprised the bulk of the settlement's concrete, though plans were now in place for several miles of paved road and the accompanying governmental implications. Merickel wished them luck.

The stop was a bust all around, offering neither information nor revenue. The lone proof of life came as an airfield maintenance truck equipped with a snowplow and an unlit but anxious rooftop light. The truck's suspension succumbed to Johnny's familiar weight leaning on the hood as he spoke with the driver about summer's welcome demise and how the secret of Gustavus was out, evidenced by all the new lodges and the corporate jets that had invaded during the last four months. The next Telluride, both agreed, though Merickel guessed neither had ever actually seen the ski town but enjoyed the tone of cynicism.

The driver, introduced as Greg, gave Merickel's task the requisite exhalation of respect. He remembered Linda but shook his head at questions about Scott, recalling the man like a seasonal bird he might have noticed in the past but would not think about until its return. Greg smiled when Merickel said to call if he heard anything.

"That's why I live here, officer," he said. "I don't want to hear anything for the next six months."

He promised to contact the bananas' owner before the bears or her neighbors got to the boxes and rolled away with the clunky stride of a state-maintained transmission.

Smoke trails hinted at warm lives below as the Beaver climbed off Gustavus and turned south, trees thinning to beach sand and then cold green water under the floats. Merickel studied the eddies and currents with a meditative stare he hoped to retain for the entire ten-minute trip to Hoonah.

"You hanging in there, Joe?"

The words crackled through Merickel's loaner headsets. After listening to Johnny swap weather and position reports with other pilots all morning he wondered if the impersonal equipment allowed such unofficial communication.

"Just collecting my thoughts."

Johnny put a thick hand on the dash and eyed some showers to the west. "Can't be easy with how you and Linda go back."

"It's my job."

"Yeah, yeah, yeah..." Johnny skipped the syllables like a rock on flat water, the last one not loud enough to key the hot mic. "But still, it isn't so much the labor as the personal shit that can be tough, right? I mean, I jump in this thing, I know what's going to happen and what I need to do to get through the day. But at home...maybe I thought Margie and me would get something back with the girls gone, you know?"

"It can be work."

The intricacies of northern Chichagof Island rolled by outside Merickel's window. Varicose logging roads crawled over the hills, and without looking up he knew straight ahead lay the sheltering rise from which Hoonah took its name. Again the headset buzzed.

"It's like she and I just work around each other, and I guess it's just scary to think this might be my best shot. My only shot." The plane grumbled but settled into a descent when Johnny tweaked the throttle. "I think these things but don't feel I can tell her, you know? Her or anybody..."

The silence hung too long to be his headset cutting out, and Merickel recognized himself at a critical point. Wasn't Johnny asking a little much? This was Merickel's first time home in years, and on a morning that so occupied his mind. He could only admit negligence with a hollow nod.

Johnny shifted behind the yoke. "I'm sorry, Joe. I don't mean to be hanging my laundry out for you to see."

Merickel held up a forgiving palm and returned to his window. He had long relied on his personality to keep him free from such interactions, anonymous personnel evaluations in the military ranging from "*distant*" to "*warms slowly, but always professional.*" Merickel never disputed them, sensing either futility or hints of the truth. He took an odd pride in the silent and methodical way of working through things that he and Jan had established long ago without words—a bad day or her woman problems earned a firm hug or kiss atop the head, allowing a taste of her scalp. Maybe he put too much faith in his touch, but he trusted that more than his tongue. Perhaps the cost was a certain passion, but at what price peace?

* * *

Merickel had chuckled when he first heard rumors of his hometown making an effort at tourism—quaint guest houses, wine lists on menus, and charter cruisers with leather seats for Outside anglers in their fresh Cabela's gear. Despite such endeavors, the village he and Johnny passed over looked familiar enough to make his blood sing with an anxious twinge, and Hoonah's intrinsic industries—the dormant cannery, unpainted workboats and restless logging equipment—hinted from the fringes how a poorly-aimed word or look might earn some vacationer an authentic experience not advertised in the brochure.

A crowd unnatural for October bordered an inner slip of the harbor as Johnny and Merickel tied up the DeHavilland. On shore the chrome of a new fire engine reflected as much of the day's overcast light as possible, dropping a diesel purr across the flat water while volunteer firefighters snugged up ill-fitting helmet straps and stiff uniforms despite a complete lack of smoke or flames. Several faces struck Merickel as familiar, though he may have just been recognizing bloodlines.

"I guess we'll just join the gawkers," Johnny said.

The slip held a twenty-nine-foot Bayliner submerged almost to her deck and oddly at peace. At the slip's head an angry young man huddled under a thick blanket emblazoned with *Hoonah Department of Public Safety*. An earring flashed behind his wet shoulder-length hair like temperamental lightning.

"I mean, what the fuck are we paying a harbormaster for anyway?" He sat flanked by an older fireman and paramedics diagnosing whether his profanity was chronic or just a symptom of hypothermic exposure.

"He can't be here twenty-four hours a day, Corey." The fireman looked up enviously at his cohorts toying with the new truck's gadgets.

"Well, maybe he should be. I've got half a mind to sue the city. And where were all these damn looky-loos this morning?"

The boy's architectural cheekbones framed a scowl that probably made more girls swoon than an average guy's smile did, and Merickel understood why his boat sinking drew a crowd.

"Is he a Sampson?"

"The baby," Johnny said. "His brothers were running around during your time, right?"

"They were."

"Well, this one is no different."

People began fracturing off to take unofficial tours of the new fire engine or check on their own boats. The more worn vessels lay relegated in distant slips while large arrows painted in caution yellow waited to guide next year's tourists to expensive summer craft. Shiny cleaning stations ensured vacationers would not need to kick innards off the dock or clean their crab on a cleat. Merickel was considering how to best approach Corey Sampson when a fisherman sidled up to Johnny without eye contact.

"Hey, Westwind, you gotta move your bird."

He pointed at a cabin cruiser slipping past the jetty with a far less sleek craft in tow. Johnny had his airplane slid back to allow the two boats berth before Merickel noticed the name stenciled on the second vessel's stern. He could not imagine how long he would have stood and stared had Johnny not put a hand on his shoulder.

"We need to talk, Joe. In private."

* * *

The *Following Sea* appeared unaware of her key evidence status. A bag of Ruffles—empty and folded in half—lay across a laminated desk map as the lone sign of inhabitance in the wheelhouse. The deck suggested nothing more than honest hard labor, bearing only scars of past burdens and paint chips waiting like leaves for the slightest disturbance to free them. A flash of the badge got them aboard, but Merickel could not have felt less official standing on her planks.

"They found her anchored up around Flynn Cove," Johnny said after conferring with the cabin cruiser's skipper. "The tanks are low but the reserve jugs would've got him farther."

"If he were really running."

Johnny slumped like a country doctor agreeing with some dirt farmer's self-diagnosis. He took the captain's chair under a creak of protest and swung a few degrees.

"You know this run through the strait we're on, Joe? Well, I think Scott is on the same run."

His eyes warned of shaky ground ahead, but Merickel nodded permission to continue.

"Listen, I know you thought real highly of Linda, and God knows she was the sweetest girl. But I heard things." Johnny dropped the paint flakes he was playing with. "I'm not holding out anything, Joe, but I know she could be a flirt. It's natural, I guess, being one of the only girls in a mostly boys' game. Guys talk, and word was there were others besides Scott."

"Any idea who?"

Johnny gave a welcome shrug.

"I don't think even the loose lips knew. She took extra time on this run, laid over for weather more often. Sometimes when she had no passengers coming back into town, I'd let her keep the plane out for the night. I got the idea she was staying out here because of someone."

Merickel contemplated the familiar cut of Port Frederick off the bow, where decades earlier he had regularly escaped far smaller problems than today's in his father's skiff. Clouds now stole the taller mountains at the inlet's far west end.

"Someone like Dan Gilbert?" Merickel said. "Or this Sampson?"

"Honestly, I think if either were the one Scott wanted, talking to them wouldn't be an option." Johnny ran a hand through his thick hair and stood. "I just hoped you and I might come across Scott chugging along or the Coast Guard would find him run up on some rocks, so you wouldn't have to drag through this shit and maybe see a side of Linda you didn't want to."

Merickel should have offered his friend an absolving wave, but just stared at a neglected Chris-Craft in a neighboring slip that longed to sink rather than suffer further indifference.

"It's appreciated, Johnny, but all this was going to come out in the wash anyway."

A late-model Blazer now sat atop the ramp, wearing mud streaks and the distinctive grizzly bear logo of the Hoonah Police Department. Merickel glanced at his watch.

"How long have we got?"

Johnny stood to study some aspiring weather to the west. "I need to call the office, see if there's anything we need to pick up or drop off out in Pelican or Elfin. I can give you at least an hour, maybe a little more."

Merickel took over the swiveling chair freed by his friend.

"An hour, then."

* * *

Three summers ago Merickel was more or less guaranteed the chief of police job in Hoonah had he chosen to apply. He had politely declined the informal offer and the current department head was supposed to know nothing about being second choice. The hastily-constructed smile presented on the dock by Chief Hayes, pushing fifty and thick in a way the uniform made look muscular, hinted there had been a leak. The two officers shared a cursory inspection of the *Following Sea,* revealing nothing new. The harbor-master assured them he would allow no one aboard and they drove the pot-holed half-mile to the police station immersed in conversation that carried less weight than pure silence.

Like its Skagway counterpart, the Hoonah police station had come into this world with different aspirations. Skagway's city hall building began as a short-lived women's college, Hoonah's jail as a failed retail store whose inventory no one remembered, though Merickel still expected a bell to ring upon entering. Hayes introduced him to Corey Sampson with a jerk of his head. Supplementing the wool blanket with a thick Alaska Marine Highway mug, the young buck sat in a caster-wheeled chair across the desk from an officer with a high-and-tight. Freshly ex-military, Merickel assumed, and already regretful of separating.

Sampson laughed into his coffee cup. "How many times do I have to tell this shit?"

"Until we get bored," Hayes said in all caps. This could not have been his first go-round with the young man.

Sampson had returned late last night to the boat he lived on, unapologetically drunk. Noises topside woke him shortly before sunrise and he had retrieved a 9mm from under his bunk. Fully registered, he boasted, reinforcing Merickel's belief that those least worth killing always defended themselves the best. The hung-over Sampson soon found himself blindsided, disarmed and duct-taped to a chair below deck. Sampson now dismissed Sounder's hits as bitch-slapping, and thanks to repeated tellings had somehow twisted the interrogation into a debate he had won.

"What did he want?" Merickel pulled out his notepad. The word *stairs* greeted him from within a loose circle.

"He wanted to know if I'd been screwing his girl."

"And?"

Sampson's snide laugh made Merickel jealous of Sounder's chance to smack the kid around.

"Hey, some psycho's beating on you, of course you're going to say you never touched her."

"But did you?" Merickel wrote *did you* on his pad.

Sampson shifted.

"I don't have to answer that."

Merickel sighed. "So you might have had all this coming then?"

Sampson stuck out his AMH mug for Hayes to refill.

"I could've had her, man. Easy. She would stop by the harbor packed into those jeans, saying how we should take my boat out some time." Sampson's search for empathy bypassed Hayes and High-and-Tight before settling on Merickel. "You know the type—all talk, no follow-through. I would bet that's what sent Sounder over the edge."

He stopped when six eyes confirmed he had overstepped himself, and sipped coffee before finishing his story. Sounder had used a gaff to pound a sloppy hole in the fiberglass hull, leaving Sampson gagged in the quarters below before stealing his adjacent Boston Whaler to tow behind the *Following Sea*. The lines were loosened only enough to drop the bow a couple feet and frighten Sampson, but his struggle with the chair had landed the still duct-taped young man on his back in a foot of water, risking hypothermia. Sampson's yells were not heard until almost noon, when some boat owners arrived at the dock after a lazy Saturday late-breakfast.

"It doesn't sound like you were the one he was looking for," Merickel said.

Sampson shed the heavy blanket. "Well, I know I'm not the only one she wagged her ass at, and not everyone has my discretion."

"Did you hear of anyone else?" Hayes struck an unnaturally thoughtful pose only the worst B-movie director would ask him to assume.

"Not names," Sampson said. "But you heard stories."

Merickel pocketed his notepad.

"That'll do for now," he said. "Chuck?"

Hayes gave a terse headshake and stroked his chin.

"You can go now, Corey, but we'll be in touch."

Sampson rose.

"Sounder better hope you find him first, because if my brothers and I get to him..."

This threat trailed off under implications of a boatload of gun-toting has-beens trolling the shoreline and an insurance settlement that would mellow Sampson's anger into little more than a good anecdote to tell next June on the *Crazy Wind II*. Merickel estimated Sampson to be at least twenty-five, and despite strong genetics and local credentials his sun was setting. The smarter high school girls were doubtlessly already declining offers of free beer, and a sinking in his home harbor would not help.

Merickel took down a number for Sampson's parents and talked a few minutes with Hayes and High-and-Tight, figuring it bad form to dash out right away. He thought of a UFO crashing in some farmer's field—the G-men might sit down for a slice of the wife's pie, but Merickel did not need to show all his cards just because something landed in Hayes's backyard.

All present agreed the missing Boston Whaler was stout enough but anywhere outside Cross Sound would be suicide in swells this time of year. Hayes was bursting to contact the law down in Angoon and Kake, while High-and-Tight used the second line to alert the Coast Guard of the newly-recovered *Following Sea* and freshly-stolen Whaler. Merickel excused himself via hand gestures to find a payphone to check in with Bench.

The dock's phone was in use by a denim-clad teen determined to get his quarter's worth. Down below Merickel saw Johnny sitting on his float with a familiar form facing him—hands pocketed, arms bowed outward, knees bending only for physical punctuation. The green jacket was new, but Merickel knew the cap read *Husqvarna* before its owner turned toward him with a fond disappointment as he approached. The man's words fell through a cracked smile.

"Well, well, well..."

Merickel swallowed to get his throat working.

"Hey, Pop."

* * *

The weather out towards Elfin Cove and Pelican was down. Johnny had radioed with a Ward Air pilot who turned around out near Lemesurier Island, reporting fog and drizzle to the water. He dug into his pocket for a note.

"Turns out I actually had a passenger out in Pelican."

Word of Sounder had gotten through the rain and now one of the lodge's cooks was eager to leave despite a week left on his contract. Merickel studied the name scrawled on the torn corner of a phonebook page bearing some familiar numbers, then slipped the paper into his wallet behind the ticket stub from the other night's magic show.

"They're all holed up in the main building for the night," Johnny said. "I'm heading back to Juneau while the weather's still good, but promised to try at first light and said you would call him."

Merickel imagined the small crowd huddled in the locked lodge out in Pelican with rifles not cocked for years, enjoying a different kind of Saturday night.

"So I'll call your dad's place in the morning and pick you up on the way." Johnny averted his eyes—the old man had probably been working on him for a half-hour, and any protest now would paint Merickel as ungrateful and too big for his roots. Johnny had the DeHavilland taxiing out before father or son spoke.

"I'll have to clean off the spare bed." Ed Merickel's voice sounded husky. A fall cold, maybe, but most likely smoking again.

"The couch is fine. I don't want to impose."

Ed's eyes gleamed in a way only his wife had known how to defuse. His boy wished she were there to do so.

"You were an imposition for eighteen years, and now you're concerned?" He climbed the ramp with a walk stiff from numerous little accidents rather than a single large one. "Let's get home before we get soaked."

Merickel toyed with sentiments about why he had not called first, but they all sounded like someone offering repairs to damage the other party would otherwise not have noticed.

"I'm sorry about the Walker girl." The old man looked straight forward, preferring to keep emotion in his peripherals. "You shouldn't be on the case, like how doctors can't operate on family."

"It's my job, Dad."

Ed now eyed him directly—skepticism could be faced head on. "Sometimes a job comes second to being a person, Joe."

A lone 80's K-Car waited in the gravel lot, her once excited red beaten to a submissive maroon. The car seemed to rattle without even running.

"Where's the truck?" Merickel said.

"At home." The driver-side door pleaded for WD-40. "I bought this from the oldest Weldon boy when he left to live with his mom in Spokane. Saves gas money. And there's a cassette player, but I got no tapes so I don't know if it works."

Ed didn't hide the butts in the ashtray and a small scented mirror tree was losing the battle. A sticker on the dash proclaimed *Hey, it runs.*

At the grocery store Merickel found the selection greater and the aisles smaller than he remembered. He received a few hellos from faces he had seen earlier on the dock, as being in tow of his dad jarred memories. The old man selected a six-pack of Black Label with a challenging glance, but Merickel just feigned interest in some hyper-flavored corn chips. At the counter Ed waved his son's wallet away and mumbled something about guests in his home.

The house Merickel grew up in passed by without discussion behind fogged windows. Four years ago a couple from Bellingham bought the property and started the Port Frederick Bed and Breakfast. Aside from a long-gone mention of the old place being whored out by yuppie snowbirds, his father now declined comment. Ed's new residence lay up in what had been Merickel's playground of trees and trails. The homes ranged from prebuilt boxes like Ed's to double and single-wides that had crawled up the hill with their owners. The yard they parked in was the type most hid beneath an overturned skiff, auto project or a firewood pile. After this week's rain a misstep off the plywood path would sink a person ankle deep.

"I'd have figured higher ground would keep me drier," Ed said. "But I guess that's the price for a view."

Inside Ed gave a tour with finger points while unloading groceries. The unmade bed said he had risen late and a comforter on the couch suggested several hours lapsed before his showering and heading to the dock. If Merickel's father was smoking again he kept it a secret from the house.

"You want some toast?"

Merickel said no and located the faded Olympia Beer wall clock he knew hung somewhere in the house—3:48. He set his duffel down and took the phone's being buried somewhere out of view as a sign that his call to Bench could wait a little longer. Ed locked in a couple slices of white bread and began rummaging around the couch.

"I was clearing out some closets and wanted to see if you were interested..."

Ed pulled on the comforter, causing a pistol underneath to drop with a metallic snap on the coffee table, chipping further a long-defeated finish. He picked up the Ruger .41 Blackhawk Flattop and held the gun supine for his son.

"...in this, I mean. If you wanted it."

Merickel forced himself to take the gun casually, not as he had been taught to disarm a suspect. As a child he had only seen the Ruger holstered and wrapped in a cloth beneath his parents' bed. The chambers were empty, but the safety off.

"You don't need it?"

Ed answered his toast's pop.

"Ammo is getting expensive, especially with that off caliber. And

I've still got my .38 for protection. I thought you might like this one for work."

"They're pretty strict on our side arms, Dad..."

"For yourself, then. For Christmas."

Merickel would not think of the old man's gift for two more months and then it would be a quick trip to the hardware. Despite a burnt dryness the toast looked delicious. Ed pushed the loaf his way and made for the couch and TV. Merickel wondered what observations and conclusions Lambar or Bench might draw from this aging widower leaving a sloppy wake of guns and beer and cigarette butts, when in actuality they would just be looking at someone who had lost the person who cleaned up after him.

When the cancer took Merickel's mother five years ago, it also took an orderliness that, along with a strong jaw and feet a little too wide for regular shoes, had been her son's principal inheritance. Merickel did not doubt his mother had loved his father, but also assumed that at some point she lumped him in with the weather and garbage bears and other things that life's structure must be adjusted for and worked around. Ed had logged his native Washington until creeping bureaucracy and a restless personal compass drove him north. The profession demanded some honest hell-raising, though his stories of youthful adventure and debauchery always struck his son more as cautionary tales of poor judgment. After kicking around the camps he was lucky enough to land a Hoonah girl who eventually gave him a boy. The elder Merickel had probably wanted to fall right into a *Father Knows Best* role, but his occasional binges and mercurial moods often found Ed getting the talking-to at each episode's end. What little hope he gained when his boy signed up first as a deckhand then for the Army faded after Joseph returned from both just as uptight and milquetoast as he left. After his wife passed and the 1990 Tongass Timber Reform Act put the logging industry into a nosedive, Ed Merickel slipped into a half-assed retirement. Since his wife's passing, father and son communicated primarily on birthdays and federal holidays, approaching each other less as disappointments than as genetic curiosities.

They called home over the toast and an early dinner of Chunky soup and Triscuits, Ed giving each of the grandkids a round and Jan soothing Merickel with the sweet monotony of laundry, inconvenient cramps and time-outs. Even the relayed message from Lambar came like raindrops on a leak-free roof.

"I told him if you were in Hoonah you'd be at your dad's," Jan said.

After saying goodbye Merickel steeled himself with a glance at the clock—4:53. He released a calming breath on the department phone's fourth ring and eventual click of the machine. He left what stark details he considered adequate, his father's phone number and a pledge to call from Pelican, and then joined the old man on the couch. What entertainment Ed's tiny dish pulled down through the clouds came from places where people went out on Saturday night. The blinds for the big window behind the TV remained open even after daylight faded, and when the set fell to darkness on commercial breaks Merickel saw shadowy outlines of the bay below.

"The kids sound good," Ed said. "Maybe I'll make a trip up for the holidays."

"Anytime," Merickel said. "I want to give the other guy some time off around Christmas, so I might be pulling a few double shifts."

He tried to hide the hint, but a raised brow said Ed would not push the point.

"We'll see. Maybe I'll go see your uncle down in Astoria. Or Joe

Dolan wants to sell his boat and head to Costa Rica. Says we could live like kings on a thousand bucks American per month, maybe do a little charter stuff on the side."

Merickel mused, thinking of his father as tropical royalty among the bugs and third-world cleanliness.

"How about you?" Ed said. "How long you going to watch over complaining tourists and shoplifting cruise ship workers?"

Merickel drummed his fingers. "Jan's happy, the school is good for the kids. Summers are a little crazy but survivable."

Ed spread out like a tired eagle. "We're getting a few tourists here now. No doubt you've heard we need policemen."

Though Merickel's refusal of the Hoonah job was not supposed to have left the room, plenty of people had walked in and out of that room since then.

"I like it there."

"I don't doubt that. Don't doubt it at all."

When Merickel went to the fridge he expected to find the last Black Label clinging to the empty plastic rings, but three remained. Beer was getting stronger or the old man weaker. He plucked a Pepsi and studied the Braves home game schedule on the fridge door.

"You know your grandfather still thought you were overseas when I visited him last winter," Ed said.

"I saw him right after I left the Army, Dad, when I was going through the academy in Sitka." Merickel recalled the withered old man in the Pioneer Home, trying to pull memories or interest from a web of six kids and too many interchangeable grandchildren. The encounter had inspired cards bearing photos rather than repeat visits.

"You still need to think of family and your heritage." Ed settled on some syndicated sitcom that had taken the public too many seasons to realize wasn't funny. "If only so the kids know where they came from."

This from someone who had sat through his wife's tribal functions with the dull stare most people reserved for church or graduation. After Ed stopped going his wife's attendance waned like eroding shoreline—one year it was only five potlatches, three the next, and finally casseroles sporadically dropped off with apologies for not being able to stay.

"The kids know, Dad, but I'm also making my own life."

"I suppose." Ed rose for another beer, dropping his words into the open fridge. "Maybe your job can't allow a person to have too much history with a place, you need to be some kind of robot..."

"It requires objectivity," Merickel said. "Removing yourself from the equation."

Ed retook his seat. "And you think you can do that?"

"It's my job."

Ed let a thumb-sized glob of foam creep down the can, sensing his boy's urge to catch the mess.

"So they know? Jan knows?"

Merickel plucked a nearby tissue, averting a look to break the old man's balls. Ten years ago. Merickel was stationed in Germany and engaged to Jan who waited stateside when his mother wrote to say Linda was getting married, a real whirlwind thing with some guy from Yakutat. Merickel dropped the week's pay he had been saving for the rehearsal dinner on a last-minute ticket and told his CO that a family emergency had arisen at home. He made the mistake of calling his dad from the airport, where he got the riot act at international rates. After tearing up the nonrefundable ticket he walked narrow foreign streets until dawn. Damning time zones, he had called from a payphone only to hang up when he got Linda's machine. Any message left would be like busting into the wedding and then being directed to take a pew. Linda's planned union dissolved with no hard feelings, and the old man had since held on to the incident like a left jab Merickel always saw coming but could not block.

"Wouldn't serve a purpose," he said. "Except for those who like to stir the pot."

Ed looked comfortable in his chair's home-field advantage.

"Figures it'd be one like her to pull the stick from your ass." *One like her.* The old man waited for his son to beg for some sort of clarification—the very reason Merickel did not—and his rocking head betrayed a slipping tolerance. "I mean, she was a sweet gal, but she had you, Joe, from the time you were both small. Had you in that way…I've been there, kid, and can't fault you."

A *Cheers* rerun came on and Merickel pulled the Pelican kid's number from his wallet. He held up the paper like a lottery ticket that meant a small win for both of them.

"Can I use the other phone? Business."

Ed pointed toward the bedroom. "Don't worry about the charges. My treat."

Despite the room's predictable disarray, an innate warmth tempted Merickel to lie down. He used his calling card and asked for the name—Brad Unger—giving his title immediately. The voice was vulnerable and offered no new information. The college boy up from Vermont for the summer had developed what he now discounted as a mere crush on the friendly female pilot fifteen years his senior. He was sorry he couldn't offer any more insight on Scott Sounder but just wanted to catch the southbound jet tomorrow with his gnarly tale to share in the faraway safety of some student union. Unger listed the precautions they had taken—secured doors, jury-rigged trip wires and so on. Merickel gave his approval and promised to see him in the morning.

The old man lay asleep in his chair, a hand guarding the remote. Merickel watched another twenty minutes of TV before closing the blinds and securing the house. He laid a comforter over his father and took the couch, intent on letting his mind burn itself out like a fire he had over-fueled.

* * *

The phone woke Merickel at 7:10, two hours after Ed dragged himself to the toilet and disappeared into his bedroom. The female voice on the line was unenthused about working Sundays and said Johnny had just taken off. Ed's blinds were losing their battle with the dawn and Merickel cracked them to find a high overcast that even risked sun breaks.

He packed his bag before showering and emerged from the bathroom to find his father's bedroom door ajar. Ed sat on the mattress edge, the covers around his midsection and bare legs draping to socked feet. He still wore the previous night's flannel shirt and a chill could not be denied.

"Morning, Dad."

"Johnny must be on his way." Without surrendering his cocoon Ed hunted for more clothing. "I'll give you a ride."

"You rest. It's nice out and all downhill to the dock."

Ed welcomed this but still shifted.

"So out to Pelican and then home, eh?" he said. "I'll call next week and we can set something up for the holidays."

"That'd be good." Merickel shouldered his bag. "Thanks for putting me up."

Ed made a quick search for some trinket or talisman to send with his boy. He came up with only a wave.

"Be safe, Son, okay?"

Merickel promised he would and left his father's house into a morning that was a true gift for October. The remnants of those days of rain coated Hoonah like sweat after virtuous work. Wherever Sounder found himself now, the chilly air and good visibility had to hit like the sun rising on an all-night drunk that darkness had made seem eternal.

The old man was getting better. In the past Merickel would not have escaped Ed's house without attempts to rectify the night before, to jam thirty-five years of misaligned cogs into several sloppy sentences and a clumsy handshake. Merickel still expected the eventual apologetic phone call and other small aftershocks that he could face when they did arrive, though he hoped they would not come too soon.

Johnny's form dominated the ramp overlooking the harbor. He leaned against the rail, scowling at his airplane or the mountains or just the whole mess in general. Merickel hoped the big man's mood had broken with the weather, but the first look he offered did not bode well.

"I'm sorry, Joe."

Johnny tipped his head down toward the dock, never un-pocketing his hands. Two stiff forms stood below next to his tied-up DeHavilland like poles supporting dark overcoats.

"They bought tickets and were waiting. I think they're pissed, but with these guys who can tell?"

One had to be Bench. Merickel had assumed the trooper was in Skagway all day yesterday, when he had actually been bound back to Juneau. They likely were not here for moral support.

"They say anything?"

Johnny shook his head. He had not showered and appeared regretful.

"They asked about yesterday and I told them what I knew. The basics, I mean, what we came up with."

Merickel retook his bag and started down the ramp.

"Is it going to be a long flight?"

"Not if I can help it." Johnny laughed. "I'll run the motor balls out and burn her up if it gets this done with quicker."

The troopers didn't look at Merickel or even each other as he and Johnny approached. Whatever plan they had was long finalized. He stopped just short of handshake range and said good morning.

"Hello, Chief Merickel." The taller one was deep into his forties but could probably take on any new recruit. His jawline would make both women and geometry teachers take notice. "I'm Trooper Bench and this is Trooper Grubbs."

Nowhere near as tall or angular as his partner, Grubbs compensated with intensified staring and an abrupt nod that could have passed for a nervous tic.

"I hope your time in Skagway went well," Merickel said.

"Just fine," Bench said. "I was able to spend the better part of Friday and yesterday morning at the scene and doing interviews. I left yesterday afternoon when the weather lifted and it sounded like we might have something out here." He unclasped his hands and used the one bearing a large academic ring to signal down the dock. "May I speak with you privately?"

Bench led Merickel behind a winterized cabin cruiser to a location he had in all likelihood scouted out upon landing.

"Could you please explain, Chief Merickel, what you have been doing the last two days?"

"Investigating the case, interviewing witnesses." Bench's face told Merickel the man had been trained not to interrupt. "My job, I thought."

"It concerns me," Bench said. "That you were making this trip, talking to persons of interest, without keeping us involved."

"Things developed rather quickly."

"Part of your job is controlling that pace." Bench scanned the nearby boats. "You spoke with two people who had direct contact with Sounder and we were never notified or kept appraised of the new information they offered."

Merickel straightened but still felt somehow hunched.

"I assumed Hayes's call to you yesterday would suffice as an update. And I wanted to meet with this Unger kid in Pelican to see where that led, to make sure it was solid."

The trooper's look said they both knew better.

"I understand Mr. Lester's theory about Sounder's possible motives and course. Hopefully Mr. Unger can shed a little more light." Bench crossed his arms. "But we don't think your presence is necessary. We can handle the matter from here."

He pulled an envelope from his raincoat.

"You are booked on the L.A.B. flight home at 9:30. Get a receipt for the cab to the airstrip and you will be reimbursed."

Merickel took the ticket. "Thank you, but can I ask why?" The muscles of Bench's jaw contracted. "I saw in your file that you served. As did I. Marine Corps, eight years."

"Permission to speak freely, Mr. Bench."

"We don't feel you are the best person for this case, Mr. Merickel." Bench's tone stayed concrete enough to chip teeth. "Frankly, your procedures are lacking, you do not seem interested in working as a team, and you were not clear about your involvement with the victim."

Merickel cracked his mouth for a wordless protest but Bench continued.

"An officer's first murder investigation should not be a long-time friend. In short, I think you are in over your head."

"I am chief of police." Even Merickel recognized his own tone as less defensive than workman-like, moving their conversation to a welcome end. Bench uncrossed his arms in a gesture most would take as combative, but for the trooper almost reached sympathy.

"I've seen this before, Mr. Merickel. People enjoy strolling around with the badge, smiling and maybe citing local kids for breaking curfew. Andy Griffith and Mayberry stuff. Then something happens and they can't become real lawmen. In your career—military and civilian—have you ever drawn your weapon in the line of duty?"

Until now this had been a source of pride. "No, sir."

"Please fax your report to my office by tomorrow afternoon," Bench said. "Also, I noticed you have some vacation days coming up this week."

Merickel made him wait a couple beats before saying yes.

"I suggest you take them." Bench glanced at the water and motioned that Merickel could leave the slip. "Finally, I would like to compliment you on Officer Lambar. He was very professional and helpful, despite being close to Ms. Walker."

"I will pass that along. He'll be happy."

Johnny's face said Grubbs had already told him to plan weight and balance for three rather than four. Minutes later, Merickel didn't even look up from the payphone when the big Pratt & Whitney rumbled across the sound.

* * *

Merickel shared the L.A.B. Cherokee Six with two hastily-packed boxes of furnace supplies and a hard woman the pilot dropped off in Haines on the way north. She said nothing, but he guessed her scowl was split evenly between his gender and Hoonah itself. A stout wind made the pilot earn his wages on the short leg up Taiya Inlet to Skagway, where Merickel declined the van ride to his house with a smile and took up his bag to walk the three blocks home. The north end of town calmed the wind enough to land with cool comfort on Merickel's face as he cut across the puddled ball diamond through a hole in the chain link fence.

He found the house quiet. Jan likely had everyone down at the red church, where she would hang around afterwards snacking on cookies while the children played among the pews and picked up faith through osmosis. Blankets curled before the TV and Disney video cases betrayed a sleepover. Merickel folded the comforters, organized the movies, and inspected a stack of mail offering nothing handwritten. He considered another shower—the one at his father's place either hadn't done the job or there was now more to scrub off—but decided otherwise. After jotting down a note for Jan, he pulled his Winchester .308 lever action from the closet gun safe. If asked he would say the truck needed running, though a blue cloud upon starting was the rig's only protest. The Mercantile was closed on Sunday, so he left a message for Art Lowes at home while the truck warmed up.

Even in the best light the city rifle range off the Dyea Road resembled a hastily-abandoned party, and despite a dry morning the shooting bench remained wet from the days of rain. Most of Skagway's gun owners were still in their houses of worship or sleeping off last night, and Merickel hoped to be gone before they showed up with loud music, salty snacks and freshly-drained beer cans for targets. More than the marksmanship medals and citations that his time with the Service Rifle Team had earned him, Merickel missed their range. Fort Benning had provided a sterile environment with procedures and safety equipment and an order he realized more with each passing year that he would never find elsewhere.

He laid a worn blanket on the bench and set up some old targets from the truck before slipping into his familiar shooting trance for twenty minutes that passed like five. He searched, as always, for that perfect crossroad of being locked into position but also completely relaxed. A mix of nostalgic value and brute strength, the .308 felt like performing surgery with a chainsaw when Merickel thought of the Remington under Art's glass counter downtown. Nonetheless the plates held a few groupings that made him wish he had brought a ruler. He allowed himself a minute to study them before unloading the rifle and tossing the targets under a tarp in the truck bed.

With Trooper Bench gone they were probably okay to start clearing the yellow tape whose implied urgency remained in the trees when Merickel pulled deep into the cabin's drive. He slipped the rifle behind the bench seat and secured the truck's lock, arthritic with internal rust. He was confident the spare key Linda often mentioned still remained hidden near the water meter, but he found the door open.

Deem had apparently gotten permission from Trooper Bench to disassemble some of the scene in preparation for new tenants. The bed was stripped, a dresser moved to reveal the duct-tape outline of a washer and dryer promised long ago, and the shelves cleared into some cardboard boxes. Nothing contained in the boxes piqued his interest at first. There were pens and mugs with local business logos, phone numbers accompanied by only first names, and clipped coupons for the next shopping trip to Juneau or Whitehorse. A family member would retrieve the boxes and the town would offer some sort of memorial if not the official funeral. Merickel would need to ask about all this just like any other person now. A realization that duty no longer entailed stoic indifference afforded him both disappointment and relief.

He had seen the envelope of photos when examining the cabin on Thursday and given them a cursory glance, but had to put them down after finding nothing incriminating. Now he methodically picked through several items before taking the envelope up again, sensing he would look at nothing else afterwards. The pictures covered a six-month period, a rain-filtered summer sun dominating most. There was Glacier Bay, the parade on the Fourth, the solstice party out at Seven Pastures, and Linda's favorite booths at the Southeast Fair over in Haines. All were double prints save for one of her standing near a small lake. The mountains of Chicaghof Island lay in the background, clouds hugging the ridgelines and a brightness suggesting out-of-frame sunlight. A casual observer would not notice the care taken by the photographer to exclude every hint of himself from the scene, save for the obvious fact that someone had been there to take the picture. The thought that he had missed the photo on Thursday fired a cold shot through Merickel, though he wasn't sure if the chill sprung from his previous sloppiness or what he now saw.

The closest thing to proper evidence the cabin contained, Merickel kept the lone print, placing the remaining photos back into the box and taking a seat at the small kitchen table. He would give himself half an hour. Jan might press him, albeit politely, if he was gone much longer. He did not think Deem would stop by, but even so the man's poorly-muffled F150 would grant Merickel at least thirty seconds to compose himself.

Linda smiled from the photo in a way that guys like Joseph Merickel didn't dare think existed until it was aimed right towards them, at which point nothing else existed. He hoped she had kept the other print hidden away somewhere that would never know what had happened in this cabin, somewhere Trooper Bench could never investigate, and somewhere Scott Sounder would never reach.

* * *

Lambar's Isuzu sat parked next to his chief's outside city hall. A smooth overcast seeped up from the south, promising dampness and stealing any shadows. Merickel checked his face in the rearview for signs of anything and took the steps slowly.

The junior officer sat at his computer while a nearby TV played some Sunday talking-heads show arguing politics like any of that crap really mattered. Lambar's reflexive attempt to always look just a little busier relaxed quicker than it would have last week.

"You're back."

"Yep." Merickel surveyed his own desk. "How was Trooper Bench's visit?"

"Productive." Lambar must have spent the morning agonizing over the most cutting adjective. "I learned a lot. And your trip?"

"I learned some, too." Merickel plucked up a notepad. "I'll write my report tonight and get it in the computer tomorrow so you can look it over."

"Or just drop it off in the morning and I'll type and fax everything in for you." Lambar's eyes stayed on his screen. "That way I will be familiar with your findings and you can get a jump on your vacation."

Merickel hit a switch and his small computer hummed warmly, the screen scrawling a dizzying chatter of letters and numbers.

"I was considering not going," he said. "I thought it might be good for me to be here."

Lambar turned, his forced casualness straining like a too-small shirt. "The troopers have the case now. And I can handle things for a few days."

Merickel bit on an instinct to remind the kid who had been sick and crying at the cabin not four days earlier. The PC asked for a password and he entered *Edward*, his son's middle name. The screen welcomed him with the digital equivalent of a smile. A matchbook lay near his keyboard. *The Fogcutter Bar, Haines, AK* was stenciled across the cover and only two matches remained. Merickel could not imagine Bench allowing his body such impurities.

"And Calhoun was helpful?"

"Bench actually called him." Lambar said. This readiness to shift blame gave his chief hope. "Apparently Calhoun had worked with his partner before."

Merickel clicked on his e-mail icon. No new messages.

"He wasn't here that much," Lambar said. "And, y'know, any help in a situation like this..."

His words drifted and Merickel let them go before depowering the computer.

"In that case I'll try to catch the morning flight out." He stood and held up his notebook. "So if I drop this off first thing...?"

"I'll be here at seven-thirty." Lambar's tone said his only fee might be some minor editorializing. Merickel stopped at the door. Realizing he still held the matchbook, he let it fall into a nearby trash can.

"You keep yourself good, Daniel. Okay?"

Lambar was no more skilled at receiving such exchanges than Merickel was at offering them. Were they on the same basketball team, the record keeper would be hard pressed as to who should be credited with the error.

"I'll do that, Joseph."

* * *

When Merickel reached the Skagway Air Service office the counter girl sat contemplating a burgeoning drizzle with hopes of closing early. He booked himself on the next day's ten a.m. flight and fixed a tarp over his Costco supplies after loading them in the truck bed. The market's lights a block away told him winter hours were not yet in effect, and he needed a few camping items and some ice cream that Jan would at first refuse but deservedly succumb to later.

Merickel did not know Calhoun's shift but hoped on some level to find him working. To Outsiders the sight of a former law officer running a cash register might inspire curiosity and maybe even compassion. But where the summer took all comers, Skagway's winter job market was limited yet protective. Folks touting education and refusing positions as beneath them were soon on the southbound ferry. Those who stayed and wanted to work would find employment somewhere—laid-off teachers worked in the lumberyard, skilled tradesmen took on part-time shifts at the ferry terminal, and when you were up you did not look down on anyone. You might be bagging their groceries in six months. The smile Calhoun offered said he sensed a sea change.

"We close in five minutes, Joe. Make it quick."

Merickel splurged on the more expensive Dreyer's, supplementing the carton with summer sausage, crackers and batteries before heading to the register.

"This stuff will make you soft." Calhoun's apron held its own bulge, but his arms bore a bulk served well by tight t-shirts like the *Proud Panther Parent* one he wore today.

"I'll watch out for that."

Calhoun rang up the sausage. "This for your camp out?"

Merickel said yes, admiring somehow the man's ability to make him feel like a twelve-year-old pitching a tent in his own backyard.

"Still going? Despite it all?"

"I think the troopers want me to go." Merickel hoped honesty might be the one punch Calhoun would not see coming.

"Well, they probably know best. Seventeen sixty-three."

Calhoun eyed the twenty before cracking his cash drawer. He hit a few buttons with an efficiency Merickel could appreciate and the machine churned out paper in an end-of-the-day ritual. Calhoun extracted his change and removed the till.

"You going to the council meeting this Thursday, Joe?"

"Plan to." Merickel attended all city council events, especially when waning daylight meant shorter fuses and an increased need for the keeping of civility. "Why do you ask?"

Calhoun raised a silencing finger. He finished counting the drawer and wrote *$464.29* on a sticky note. Crossing his arms, the man's grin dared Merickel to make a grab for the cash.

"All the members of the review committee will be there, and

their decision is coming up next month. If we're both there maybe we can make it something of a debate. Let them, and the public, ask questions and such. If you feel up to it."

Merickel tightened his grip on the groceries. "I suppose if the entire council says they're willing..."

"I already talked to them all and they are."

"I guess it's settled then." Seeing no quicker escape route, Merickel started towards the lazy electric doors. "I should be home late Wednesday, weather permitting."

"I want it back, Joe."

Merickel had no choice but to turn around. Calhoun's arms remained crossed, maybe even flexing a little. All this with only a rack of potato chips for an audience.

"The town needs to know they are safe," he said. "That their chief isn't afraid to get out and find this Sounder bastard. Not just go through the motions."

Calhoun had picked up this pathetic psyche job from a hundred bad movies, but it was working this afternoon. Merickel needed to get home before the ice cream melted or he tossed his badge into Calhoun's till.

"I'll talk to you Wednesday, then. Weather permitting."

When he walked outside the sky was noticeably darker than this same time last week.

* * *

Through the window Merickel saw his boy and girl sprawled in front of the TV, though Jan at least had their brains working on a game of Monopoly. Any capitalistic intentions vanished when their father entered with his boxes. The boy accompanied him to retrieve the .308, listening thoughtfully through Merickel's instructions on proper handling of the rifle. Maybe two or three Christmases from now would find a .22 under the tree to see if the shooting eye was hereditary. Jan's hug came with a potholder on one hand and notice that dinner would be ready in ten minutes. The ice cream earned an efficient kiss and the camping supplies a nod without eye contact that saved Merickel the mess of confirming he was still going.

"So, back on Wednesday?" she said.

"Weather permitting, yeah."

He returned the rifle to the gun safe and changed into some warm sweats, enjoying having business no more pressing than *60 Minutes* and composing a report full of information that the people he was writing it for already knew. They ate with the TV on but playing the news so the kids wouldn't be too distracted. The boy spoke of a charity bike rally the previous day during which he had ridden between the ferry terminal and the bridge—his known universe—three times.

"I'm going to do the race next year," the girl said. "Joe Junior promised to help me."

"Training is important, you have to stick to it," Merickel said. "You two know that Dad is going camping for a few days, right?"

The girl said yes and the boy sat up.

"I want to go. Someday, I mean."

"We'll see," Jan said.

"Someday," Merickel said.

The first segment of *60 Minutes* held his interest, but the second involved some Middle East leader whose name only became familiar in opposition to others. When Art Lowes called, Merickel placed the remote between the kids before retreating to the phone on the back porch.

"Got your message," Art said, echoes of the same show Merickel's children had selected filling the call's shadows. "I don't usually open until ten this time of year."

"Well, I'm flying out at ten and would really like to have it."

"What does a lawman want with a bolt action rifle?"

"It's not for work."

Art paused for details, but Merickel's silence assured the store owner he would have to wait for the grapevine or make them up himself.

"I ought to charge extra," Art said. "But I guess I can be there at nine-thirty. Maybe next time you or the kid catch me speeding..."

"Thanks, Art. I'll see you at nine-thirty."

Jan was folding clothes in the bedroom. Any thought she might be snooping left Merickel's mind quickly enough to make him realize the notion had never even entered hers.

"Dad might be by during the holidays," he said. "Just to warn you."

"He's doing okay?"

"Getting by."

"It would do him good to see the kids." Her half-smile suggested some sort of contact, if only the touch of a hand. "And you had a good visit?"

"I suppose." Merickel picked up a flannel shirt, weighing its worth against a light jacket better for rain. "Good as can be expected under the circumstances."

"I'm sorry the troopers took you off the case," she said. "I mean, if that's what you wanted. If not, then I guess I'm happy about it."

"It's probably for the best," he said. "This is more their specialty than mine."

"Do you think they'll find him?" Jan looked around for something to straighten, settling on some socks that already appeared in their natural order. "There's only so long he can run, right? Especially this time of year. Won't something catch up with him eventually?"

Merickel chose the warmth of the flannel and placed the shirt on his pack.

"I guess, honey," he said. "But I don't know. I wish I did but I really don't."

Jan patted the stack of clothes for physical punctuation.

"I'll let you finish packing."

He smiled. "I won't be long."

He watched Jan descend the stairs, seeing everything a normal guy had right to hope for—she did good by his children and they both knew what basically made the other happy. A fellow would be stupid to ask for more, and Merickel could almost say that any man who did not face this fact deserved whatever lesson came his way.

* * *

Merickel had ridden with the same Ward Air pilot every time since retaking his trips three years ago. He thought the stout bearded man's name was Rich, but felt their relationship now too evolved to ask. One of those lifer float-drivers who accepted their work like a hard labor sentence for some justified crime, the pilot had said little when Merickel originally showed him the place on a map and emphasized the lake as his own personal spot. Still, the man always dropped him off after the other passengers and picked him up in an empty airplane, the only emotion ever shown being his regular grumble of appreciation when Merickel slipped him a twenty upon return to Juneau. This familiar anonymity, the opportunity to be a smoky memory recalled and then forgotten over the course of a thirty-minute flight, was what sent Merickel to Ward Air over Johnny for such travel.

This morning the Cessna 185 belonged to Merickel alone and Chatham Strait revealed itself inside a frame of upslope clouds. After his flight from Skagway landed he had collected his pack and rifle and tracked swiftly through the Juneau terminal, using a high-school sports team at the Westwind counter as a buffer until outside and headed across to the Ward Air hangar. Convincing himself his avoidance of Johnny had sprung from punctuality rather than cowardice, he now thumbed through his Coonts book and enjoyed the sun breaks when they hit the Cessna's window.

Merickel's lake lay just inland of where Tenakee Inlet ate into Chichagof Island's northeast corner like a cavity too long ignored. The range to the southwest was labeled on some maps as the Moore Mountains, but he had never heard anyone call them by a proper name, much less mention them at all. Merickel had discovered the spot his seventeenth summer when, with no car to drive or mall to wander, he was left with his dad's Mercury-driven 12-foot Lund and "no open water" as the lone restriction. He had taken the Lund overnight up Port Frederick as far southwest as possible and continued on foot with a pack and bedroll, reaching the lake after a solid day of hiking through muddy clear cuts, washouts and overgrown roads. Linda always said the lake was one of those places you did not know you were looking for until it lay right under your boots.

Though the basin could accommodate a floatplane, Merickel always had the pilot drop him at the north end of Tenakee Inlet. From there he hiked the half-mile in on a rutted trail that long ago began life as a logging road before the death of all its destinations. The pilot's parting words today confirmed the man had connected the dots.

"Looks like you'll have company," the pilot said. "I saw the Forest Service plane up at your lake when I flew down from Elfin Cove earlier this morning."

Merickel's shrug fell short of total indifference.

"They don't usually bother me," he said. "They normally just tie up and head in to some research cabin they've got a couple hours to the west."

The man offered him an atypical grin.

"Just don't let those Nature Nazis tell you how to enjoy the outdoors, okay?"

Merickel helped him launch from the sloppy shore and the pilot rocked his wings passing overhead eastbound. The moist path retained his detailed footprints the several times he stopped to look back and catch his breath. He was getting soft and entertained thoughts of a fitness regimen when he returned home. If Calhoun got his way Merickel would have some free time and exercise might salvage a certain structure. At worst the market would need a checker.

Upon arriving he aligned the tent in his usual location with what he estimated was the lake's axis and tightened the lines until he considered bouncing a coin off the flanks. Alongside his sleeping bag went a small clock and supplies—canned, freeze-dried and finally crackers. Despite no real hunger Merickel pulled some Ritz and cheese slices from the tent and sat on a rock, eating and studying the squalls muscling around the passes. Weather permitting, pilots had a straight shot from there through the hills to Elfin Cove to the northwest and Hoonah to the east. Several times he heard a thumping echo he assumed to be the Coast Guard out of Sitka looking for Sounder. Merickel never saw the helicopter, and guessed that with the drier weather and depending where a guy made landfall, two days worth of solid hiking would get him to the lake, maybe a little longer if his last real meal was five days prior.

The Forest Service turbine Beaver sat moored to a tree only a five-minute hike through marshy shore and sinkholes from Merickel's camp. The polished metal and strong lines stood against the water and brush like some billboard in an empty field announcing a forthcoming shopping center or business park. Only a small USFS tree symbol on the tail betrayed any allegiance, an oddity for a service so in love with patches and emblems, and the streamlined cowl hung before all that 1940's engineering like a collie nose on a bulldog. A more powerful turboprop replaced the original piston engine, Linda had explained during one of their times here, burning jet fuel instead of regular gas and dragging the blocky workhorse through the air a little faster and farther than her original designers ever dreamed. The plane rocked under his weight when Merickel stepped on the float to peek inside. A refurbished interior boasted new instruments and radios and charts that in the right hands could carry a person far away. That same person might consider the plane's merely being there to be the ultimate good luck if he believed in such things.

The morning's transaction with Art had gone thankfully smooth. Merickel had arrived at 9:20 to grant the Mercantile owner a few extra minutes to pester him for details and was out the door with the rifle and two boxes of shells fifteen minutes later. Back at his tent, he now held the Remington like a drunk attempting eloquence at a social toast. The last five years had found too many slick semiautomatics and boorish pump-actions in his hands, offering limitless second chances and demanding no skill or discipline. The bolt action was his first love, and despite the five-round magazine he would chamber each round individually between shots.

Today he took a line along the valley to minimize wind, allowing himself twenty rounds to get the feel back and adjust the sights to his liking. Upon rising tomorrow he would turn his line perpendicular for ten shots with the prevailing breeze. If the wind shifted or picked up throughout the day he could spare another five rounds and still return home with five cartridges, give or take an errant shot here or there.

Merickel would have preferred regulation targets with stark primary colors standing out against the land, but settled for a small yellow cedar about thirty-five paces up the lake's shore. A few of the smaller branches would work fine. His mother's ancestors could probably supply some parable frowning on such practices, but any concerns faded with the bolt's fluid slide on his first round. A few initial shots favored the tree, low and to the right. Adjusting the Leupold, Merickel's next couple rounds brought the branches down. Like her military counterpart, the Remington was not overly showy but felt universal—any flaws were uniform and predictable.

Over some heated chili Merickel split his attention between the Forest Service plane and an aggressive shower drifting from the north that would make hiking miserable and slow. He had not heard the Coast Guard chopper in hours and retreated to read some Coonts inside the tent, where by sunset the water-resistant fabric danced in lulling agreement with the wind and rain. Like any red-blooded American boy, Merickel had dreamed of someday sleeping with a loaded gun, maybe as a cowboy on the plains or a jungle explorer. Checking the safety one last time, he now realized the gun's presence only meant a guy was somewhere he should not be or had fucked up somehow, and likely not entirely by accident. Any honest sleep would not be the result of a clear conscience, but some combination of exhaustion and surrendering to whatever was bound to happen.

* * *

Merickel awoke at 7:36 the next morning, three hours before Scott Sounder walked in from the northwest. He felt as comfortable in his sleeping bag as he had ever been, and made plans to fight circadian rhythms and sleep until noon that first day home. The tent convulsed around him and the sky outside rolled in an upset river of grey clouds on a southeast wind up Tenakee Inlet. Merickel warmed some dehydrated eggs and scrutinized how the steam off the stove disappeared over the lake. The eggs reminded him of his fondness for MREs with their compartmentalization and consistency. He wondered this morning, as he did at times, why he had left that life.

After cleaning up he selected a small tree across the lake for ten practice rounds. The first shot landed downwind but Merickel grouped the rest in an area he estimated no bigger than a clenched fist. He noted the couple knots the breeze gained over the water and put the rifle back in the tent. The wind held the rain at bay and he took up his cheese and crackers and the Coonts book, remaining outside even when sprinkles puckered the pages.

Only twenty-two pages remained when he first saw Sounder. Merickel supposed he could roll himself right down to the tent for the Remington, making his basic training drill sergeant proud, but he really just wanted to crawl back into his sleeping bag, finish the Coonts and drift off under wasted daylight. He marked his page and slipped the book into his jacket pocket.

The time spent watching Sounder navigate the brush equaled Merickel's entire previous exposure to the man. In the last five days his imagination had distorted Sounder's features—the jaw became more square, the shoulders prouder, the short hair sharp enough to cut skin. The Sounder walking toward Merickel fell short of these standards and at first glance did not look worthy of pursuit. Despite a canvas jacket and work pants he appeared lanky, a byproduct of flight and the *Following Sea*'s spare cupboards. His clean face indicated a razor found onboard or even packed in a post-homicide haste. Sounder's eyes hung a fixed ten paces ahead, as if looking up might reveal more perspective than a fellow could take in and keep walking, but his stride suggested he would still best Merickel in whatever test of strength the officer chose.

Sounder stopped short of what he took as the camp's border, his boots and pant cuffs damp. Merickel stood, inferring permission to enter.

"Hello, Scott." He held out the cheese and crackers.

"Yes, please."

Sounder's politeness and bare chin made Merickel feel more than just five years his senior. The younger man waited for his host to sit before doing so himself.

"How long have you been here, Mr. Merickel?"

"I caught a ride in yesterday." Merickel took some crackers himself. "I was in Excursion and Hoonah on Saturday with Johnny Lester."

"How's Johnny holding up?"

"Okay," Merickel said. "For being down two pilots and having to fly the milk run himself."

The mention of the Icy Strait run got a look of recognition from Sounder and some understanding was contained, dispensing with mandatory work both men had been dreading.

"Doesn't look like there will be a lot of flying today," Sounder said. "I heard the Coast Guard chopper yesterday, but not much else."

Merickel looked to the northwest. "You come down from Idaho Inlet?"

Sounder shook his head. "Up Port Frederick. I didn't think I would find anything worthwhile to the west."

"I spoke to the kid out in Pelican." Merickel had not planned on cheese and crackers for two and the snacks were going fast. "You were right."

"I figured everyone would think I was heading that way, so after anchoring the boat I just doubled back up the sound and hid the Whaler in a cove." He gestured to the hills over his shoulder but did not look back. "I laid low for the showers on Saturday night and went out on foot Sunday. I followed a few logging roads when it worked and rested where I could."

Sounder paused, as if ensuring his explanation satisfied whatever it needed to in both men.

"That's a healthy walk."

"It was a little tougher going than I'd estimated, but I had some food I took from Corey Sampson's boat," Sounder said. "And I have had some outdoors training in the past."

Merickel could think only of a TV show he had once watched about the military's pilot survival course in the desert, and here the ex-cadet was in a rainforest without a lizard to eat, a cactus to drink, or even a signal mirror. Nonetheless, the young man looked ready to trudge on after only a fistful of Ritz and cheese.

"How did you know to come here?" Merickel said.

Sounder set his remaining crackers aside and held up a pausing finger. His wrist held one of those bulky pilot watches that did calculations by the dozens and he brushed away crumbs before opening his pack in a blatant show of no ill will. Inside lay folded clothes and other indications that this man ran from the law with a strictness most could not attain in daily life. What he pulled out resembled the small video games Joseph Junior's friends had begun bringing around the house, prompting the boy to insist on one for Christmas.

"You know anything about GPS, Mr. Merickel?"

"Just the basics, from a fisherman buddy." He thought of Dale Crown and the chuckle his friend would get out of how those damn satellites were making life tough on more than just fish.

"Then you understand how pilots use it." Sounder's finger brought the gadget to life. "You program different waypoints so you can find your way back to them later, like when the visibility is down due to weather. This was Linda's GPS." He tapped the dirt beneath his boot. "And this is a waypoint. Here."

"What did you expect to find?"

"You hear stories, Mr. Merickel," Sounder said. "I disregard a lot as people trying to get you riled up or just boasting. It's probably similar with your profession."

Merickel released the thinnest chuckle possible. "The last week has shown me that there are a lot of stories I'm not privy to."

"Anyway, I didn't listen much." Sounder gave him a last look at the glowing screen before turning the GPS off. "I always assumed I would see the truth if any was there and then face that truth head on. It's like exercise—it's hard at first but eventually feels good, like getting done with a run or hike. And facing a little every day ensures everything doesn't come out all at once."

He punctuated his pause by running a hand through his hair. Merickel sat up in a way offering no argument.

"Still, emotion comes into play," Sounder said. "And makes the truth harder to see. You hear the same things a number of times, and even if you want to ignore them, numbers can't lie. Like a rattle in an engine that has otherwise been running good. Eventually that noise deserves a look."

Sounder reached into his coat pocket in a way that most lawmen would have reacted defensively to, but Merickel felt a million miles gone from any kind of lawman. Sounder brought out a duplicate of the photo in Merickel's own pocket.

"I found this."

Merickel studied the picture as if for the first time. Sounder sat between him and the tent and the Remington, but hardly looked threatening with hands pocketed and athletic shoulders slumped.

"I recognized the mountains," Sounder said. "And when I found this waypoint in her GPS I knew the photo had to be taken somewhere close to here. That smile tells me everything. I asked her about the photo and this waypoint, and then I had months of truth in front of me and her denying everything."

Merickel blew into his hands, passing blame for their shaking onto the wind. Sounder now seemed sinewy, his jaw resting on a neck like a bridge cable. Granted he'd had five days of solitude to develop this control, but his confession was not meant to garner any leniency. This was his truth.

"So you ran."

Sounder's look was that of a debate contestant who understood his opponent's point but could never embrace it.

"If that's the phrase you want to use."

"But most folks run in the straightest line possible," Merickel said. "At least if they're running *from* something."

Sounder looked uninterested in word games, his fingers interlocking like gears with no slipping.

"There were more elements involved in this than just Linda and I," he said. "People who needed to see there are consequences. I know I should have just let the world do its job, but..."

At this, Sounder's first stumble, Merickel felt drawn to help.

"The world's too subtle for most, right?"

"I'm not denying guilt," Sounder said. "But if I didn't try to balance something out, no purpose would be served."

"You wanted to teach them a lesson."

Sounder took back the picture and pocketed the shot as if anticipating a need for future use.

"Those people needed to see that actions have reactions. Repercussions."

"Those people?"

"Filler," Sounder said. "Just fumbling through life, contributing nothing and getting nothing out. People who Linda thought were in need of her help."

"But she was also with you," Merickel said. "You seem together, organized, hardly in need of rescuing."

Sounder studied his remaining cracker before chewing it down deliberately and ridding his fingers of crumbs with a swift motion.

"You served, Mr. Merickel, didn't you?"

"Yes, and Joe will do."

"Was your family military?"

Merickel thought of the old man's living room no more than twenty miles away, filled with *Ricki Lake* or *Montel* at this hour and the scant dishes from his son's visit still resting dirty in the sink.

"No."

"My dad flew F-86s at the tail end of Korea and then F-4s in Vietnam," Sounder said. "Did his twenty and then some. My following in his footsteps seemed inevitable, predestined."

Merickel imagined the Sounder household circa 1967—Dad in a buzz cut and Sansabelt pants, ready for war or golf but little in between. Mom still fit in her high-school cheerleader uniform and vacuumed wall-to-wall daily while listening to wordless music safe for all ages.

"I know about what happened," Merickel said and waited for the precise numbers, scores and statistics that had ended the aviator's Air Force career. Sounder offered none. They had to still be in there, catalogued to the decimal, burning like fresh paper cuts when he was staring at the ceiling trying to sleep. "But you could still fly, right? Outside the military, I mean."

Sounder gave his hands the look his father had probably offered when he stepped off the bus that delivered him home.

"The civilian sector is different, as you know. The order, the principles, they either aren't as strict or aren't adhered to. That's one reason I came north—it's just you and your aircraft. At least in the air. On the ground things are always different."

A squall line gaining strength to the southeast demanded their attention. This discourse was already bumping against the valley walls and surely would not fit in the tent.

"I think Linda wanted to save me from all my orderliness and structure," Sounder said. "To try and help me live outside all my own preset parameters."

Merickel nodded and folded the empty Ritz wrapper into itself several times. Linda had shown him how to say things that were not required and give gifts that had not been asked for or earned. And though he had never wanted to be saved, Merickel took comfort in knowing that escape route lay within his reach.

"So you were just another one she was helping, no different than the others."

"I don't regret what I did to those men," Sounder said. "It was commensurate with their actions."

Merickel toed the dirt. "And what was your plan for here? The same as Dan Gilbert and Corey Sampson?"

Sounder's grin confirmed playing stupid was neither necessary nor welcome.

"If you met those guys, then you saw. They were true pity cases." He tapped the photo through his jacket's canvas. "They couldn't make her smile this way."

Sounder's gaze wandered south, leaving Merickel's at his own boots.

"You aren't going to tell me his name," Sounder said. "Are you?"

Merickel did not dare raise his eyes to Sounder's. His peripherals began filling in with terrain if not entirely familiar at least defined and navigable. Every passing second made his silence ring a little more in agreement, and laid out his course a few steps further.

"Is that important?"

Sounder stiffened. "He is the reason for all of this. He should have come himself."

Merickel yearned for the additional cylinder of crackers that lay inside the tent, maybe with a few thick slices of the unopened summer sausage.

"Maybe he's not the man you think he is," Merickel said. "Maybe he is just another pity case. Or maybe he is just like you."

Sounder rose, opening a path to the tent and rifle.

"That's your estimation?"

"A guess, as good as I know you both." Merickel remained seated and looking up. "I only know that a girl who a lot of people cared about is gone and nothing will bring her back. I respect you wanting to see matters through, but maybe this doesn't have to end the way it started."

Sounder's earlier smile was gone, now a mile north on the wind.

"So how does it end? You taking me in?"

Merickel stood to find his legs surprisingly strong. The approaching weather would be on them in fifteen minutes.

"That was my plan originally," he said. "But now I wonder if all involved wouldn't be better served if things went differently. This man has worked hard to put together a life that won't hold up to everything that is going to fall out of this."

Sounder retook his seat on the rock.

"You don't think he deserves to pay?"

"Don't you think he will?" Merickel's own tone jumped up on him and he swallowed before continuing. "He knows he is responsible for setting all these things in motion, and his world will never line up again."

"What about you? Your duty as an officer to get your man?"

Finally a chance for the truth. "Honestly, Scott, I just plan to do my best to put this last week behind me."

Sounder joined him in studying the coming downpour and small waves lapping the floats of the weathervaning Forest Service plane.

"How far do you think she'd get you?" Merickel said.

"Not far, I bet." Sounder attempted skepticism but swayed in consideration. "If they came from Juneau or Sitka they wouldn't need a lot of fuel to just get out here and back."

"From my experience with governmental agencies, I'd bet they keep the tanks topped off," Merickel said. "Even if that's not the case, I would wager the Parkies have accounts everywhere and the average kid working the fuel pumps in Petersburg or Ketchikan won't know you from Adam. Do you have any cash?"

Sounder said yes. Merickel hid a shudder from the calculating mind before him and gestured with his foot to a root outcropping between them meant to represent the Boundary Ranges.

"They are looking for a guy in a Whaler on this side of the mountains." He dragged his boot east. "If a fellow could get across the hills, maybe up through Taku Inlet or the Stikine, then find a lake to put in near the Cassiar Highway and start south from there, he could be a long ways gone by the time rumors and receipts start adding up."

"What if the weather keeps me on this side?"

"There's always the coast," Merickel said. "You've got your GPS for help. And the worse the weather, the harder it will be for them to look for you."

"After that?"

Merickel tapped his toe where Telegraph Creek would lay in the dirt.

"After that it's up to you."

Sounder paced toward the water's edge, studying the turbine Beaver. He had likely estimated his wind correction for takeoff within seconds of first seeing the plane this morning.

"What about the Forest Service guys?"

"Their cabin is a couple hours in," Merickel said. "Even if they start hiking back when you take off there won't be much light left when they get here. I'll just say I assumed they had left when I was away from the camp. There's an off chance that they have a portable that could reach the Coast Guard down in Sitka, but otherwise Ward Air picks me up at noon tomorrow, so word might not get out until the afternoon."

Sounder surrendered a chuckle. "You've planned this like it was for yourself."

Merickel bit down on too many responses and hoped his face hung as blank as his thoughts.

"And what if I came back?" Sounder said. "Or let people know about this plan?"

"Then it's your word against mine and we will see where that leads. Your choice, Scott."

Sounder rubbed his chin, which now did not appear as smooth as Merickel first thought. The younger man finally eyed the weather as all pilots did, picturing themselves up in the heart of the whole mess. Sounder shouldered his pack and checked the GPS once more before studying Merickel like equipment whose utility he was weighing against the space it would take up.

"Why didn't you just shoot me when I walked in? I mean, won't my getting away mean trouble for you?"

Merickel thought of Calhoun bagging items with a renewed fervor, the date of the council meeting circled in red on his Emblem Club community calendar.

"This won't change anything that isn't bound to happen anyway."

Only then did Sounder approve, cinching his pack. Merickel respected the man ensuring how all the pieces would fall before committing.

"You need help pushing off or anything?"

Sounder shook his head. "No, sir, I've got it."

A handshake would be too honorable, and no words could be twisted to make all of this ring true, so Merickel held up a lone palm in a frozen goodbye. When Sounder was reduced to a crackling in the brush, the police chief went to his tent.

* * *

There would be stories—the kind of fodder people passed around and doubted but never challenged lest the conversation crumble in their hands. Most would assume Linda's mysterious true love never existed, and Merickel counted on his personality to keep him from ever being considered for the role. Joseph Merickel, a lover and adulterer? He had a great wife and kids, and just look at him. At one time such thoughts would have stung, but now he relied on them. He was not proud of using a hard-crafted reputation to disqualify him from a crime he was guilty of committing, but he would take this as a warning and heed it accordingly.

Merickel took up the Remington without ceremony and selected a single round from the box in the same manner. Prolonging the process would only hurt efficiency. He thought of the phrase he had so often used as an instructor to relax students—there was never just one shot, but rather just another shot.

Questions would arise, but Merickel figured he had at least most of today and maybe all night to work out details. Having seen the Forest Service plane on his previous visits to the lake and assuming Sounder had also, he would say he followed a hunch after being dismissed by the troopers. Maybe he could claim some sort of confrontation or scuffle mixed with a confession and subsequent escape, or perhaps Merickel was simply away from camp when the sound of the big turbine brought him back to find a recognizable and unrepentant Sounder taxiing out. From there options had been limited. He might even be able to link the photo to the GPS if he could salvage the unit and recall Linda's distant lesson on its workings well enough to make a case. This afternoon he would finish the Coonts and mull his story over for sharp edges and snags.

Emerging from the tent he found Sounder turning the Beaver into the wind for departure. An adjacent grouping of trees along the east bank afforded a natural blind. Merickel saw Calhoun ringing up items back home like an altar boy fidgeting with his rosary. The optimistic and cheery service shoppers received this week would slam to a halt after Thursday's council meeting. Vigilantism was more Calhoun's style, and Merickel could not deny wanting to watch the bully wrestle against this. There was a definite heroic ring, and he knew he must work to keep such things in check. He thought of his times here with Linda, what she might make of this morning, and how long the wait would be for his ride out tomorrow. He would never come back here again.

The engine sent out a whining growl as the propeller bit into the wind and Merickel checked his safety one more time. Scott, Calhoun, Bench, Lambar, Johnny, Jan, Gilbert, Sampson, even Linda—everyone disappeared, taking this last week of rain along with them. The Beaver was on step now, with less than half the lake separating them, and would be at least a hundred feet up when passing overhead. Merickel's shoulder took the rifle stock with a welcome naturalness that he hoped the other man experienced as his floats broke free of the water. He wanted Sounder to feel this and more—maybe an odd optimism, a chance for his skills to save him. Perhaps Sounder even smiled, looking down to offer thanks. Merickel did not notice. Rather he took aim on the center of the pilot-side window, rising up off the lake and past him slow and big as a summer moon.